THE HAIR DARE

FAITH KNIGHT

To all those who remember and loved the 1970s

CHAPTER 1

I t was 1973, and on the day of the Herbal Excellence Shampoo Model Search audition, three things blew my mind: 1) that my sister Mavis was going through with her scheme and that I—Camille Marconi—was caught up in it, 2) that Herbal Excellence actually came to our little town, and 3) that the line of girls was so long it wrapped around the Washington Street fountain twice. And that was no small thing considering it was pretty cold outside. The worst part was that the water from the fountain kept spraying us, and that was not cool (well, it was *cool*, but not righteous, if you get my drift).

New Castle, PA, was the home of Cascade Park, a new rock band called the Jaggerz, and my favorite restaurant, Augustine's Pizza, but not much else. I honestly expected the tryouts to take place in Youngstown, the closest real city this side of Pittsburgh. But the fat cats at Herbal Excellence wanted to come here for some odd reason. If not for that, we would've been at home watching Super Friends.

It took about an hour before the girls in front of us started walking. The audition was set up in a rented building that used to be a furniture store. The big red letters spelling out *Haney's* were still visible, along with the words "Since 1913." As old as the building looked, I could believe that.

I shivered, holding the ticket they'd passed out to each girl. Number 82. It told me that I was behind 81 other straight-haired hopefuls. But evidently it didn't faze Mavis, with her basketball-sized Afro, proudly waving her number 83 and standing on tiptoes looking for some of 'the people,' a group of semi-militant kids she hoped would cheer her on. I couldn't believe they'd psyched my sister out with their militant mumbo jumbo. The best thing I could do—as a loving, concerned sister—was to be there to console her when she got to the front of the audition line and heard, "Thanks, but no thanks."

"Put your arm down, Mavis," I said. "Everybody's staring."

She stopped momentarily, glared at me, and said,

"When I am the first Afro-wearin' foxy mama walking through that tulip garden with my Billy Dee Williams lookalike, I'll make sure I wave at all the little people from the other side of the TV screen—especially you, my sister."

Mavis is not only stubborn, she's also dramatic.

"Then answer me this," I said, pulling my Apple cap down to my brows. "What do 'the people' have to do with this contest, and why are you expecting them to show up? What kind of problem could they have with a daggone model search?"

Mavis pulled down her arm and gave me that look. "Since you insist, I'll tell you: when I laid out my plan, they thought the idea was brilliant: I am a *twin,* and my twin has straight hair. Since we look alike, *except* for our hair, proving discrimination will be much easier if the company decides to choose you."

And that's how this *whole thing* got started...

———

HERBAL EXCELLENCE NEVER, and I mean ever, used Afros in their ads, and to me, that was the whole point of it. In my opinion, this model search belonged to the Cool Jewels—my girls at school who had straight hair and an eye for all things fly. We entered the contest, too, and now Mavis was making a federal case out of something that was supposed to be fun.

The day I discovered her deception, I let her know I wasn't going to be on her side this time:

"Mavis, I *know* you didn't enter that Herbal Excellence contest knowing they never, and I mean ever, feature Afros in their ads. You think the Revolution will not be televised? Let me hip you to this: neither will *you* and that *do*."

When I said it, I was looking good in my new gangster pants, a fly baseball shirt, and my favorite platform shoes. As an added touch, I did a pimp walk around the vanity where she sat picking out her 'fro. So I politely flung my hair like Tina Turner.

Nothing.

I took a cleansing breath and went in for round two:

"Mavis. Uh, I hate to break it to you, but Herbal Excellence has already put it out there. They're into straight hair. So whatever jive 'the people' were talkin', I wouldn't take it too seriously." Then I wrapped my sisterly concern around her shoulder. "But don't worry, you know I'm here for you. Twin." I had to throw our unique bond in there. Twins are so much more than siblings.

But Mavis kept ignoring me. She never took her face out of that mirror. Just glared at my reflection with a big smirk and said, "That's what you think, smarty pants. I've got a plan to stick it to the man."

Whenever Mavis had a plan, I got worried, so my next move was to Mama. But it wasn't exactly a good time.

The den was Mama's exclusive part of the crib. Ever since the newspapers announced troop withdrawals from Vietnam, Mama maintained a ritual: as soon as she hit the door, she'd put on a couple of TV dinners for Mavis and me, then make a beeline for the set, flip it to *The CBS Evening News with Walter Cronkite,* and wait for him to take off his glasses and tell her when Daddy was coming home. He'd only been there for six months and was headed back stateside, but Mama still listened to Cronkite every night. After the news, she'd watch her favorite show, *Gunsmoke.*

It was about eight o'clock when I headed to the den, so I knew what that meant: no interruptions, especially if Matt Dillon was making eyes at Miss Kitty. From the stairs I heard Mama say, "I've been waiting all season for those two to kiss. Why don't they just get on with it?"

I'm not a math genius, but from what I'd heard, that show had been on TV since before Mavis and I were born. If they hadn't kissed by now, they probably weren't.

So I crept ever so slightly up to her and said, "Mama."

"What do you want? Can't you see I'm watching *Gunsmoke*?" Mama had on her ratty, pink slippers, and the garters of her stockings were rolled down below her knees. She was seriously relaxed, which meant I was dangerously close to feeling the back of her hand.

But I was on a mission.

"Mama," I said again.

She sighed. Then came the usual, "Lawd-have-mercy-what-is-it?"

"We have to stop Mavis from going to that audition for long silky hair," I said.

"What are you jabbering about, Camille?"

Mama was talking to me, but her eyes never left the TV. "Why would she do that? She has an Afro. Stop bothering me."

Then Mavis came down the stairs in a huff. She'd stood right between Mama and Miss Kitty.

"I *did* enter the Herbal Excellence shampoo contest, and I *am* going to win," she said, looking about as proud of herself as a militant in a protest march. "Camille is just jealous because she might not get picked."

By this time, Mama was wearing herself out trying to see around Mavis.

"Mavis, listen," I said. "When me and my girls show up with our long, luscious locks, the other contestants won't have a chance. Including you." Then I took my place in front of Mama, too, standing even *prouder* than a militant in a protest march.

Ignoring our dispute, Mama gave us that 'if-you-two-don't-get-out-of-my-face' look. Then she actually said it.

We both marched upstairs as we usually did when Mama was too into her TV shows to pay us any mind.

At the top of the stairs, I hurried around to face Mavis head-on and stopped her before she got to the vanity again because if I hadn't, she would have sat there staring into the mirror and ignoring everything I said. Why that Afro of hers needed so much picking and fluffing was beyond understanding. Even this beautiful head of bounteous hair doesn't need *that* much attention.

"Mavis," I said. "What was the point of keeping this a secret? You know the rule of twinness, not to mention how much I love that shampoo."

I had my hands on my hips again but didn't bother swinging my hair like Tina Turner. No need to rub it in.

"I kept it secret because if I told you first, you'd do just what you're doing now, complaining. But this is *not* all fun and games, Camille; I'm on a mission."

She had her hands on *her* hips, but she looked more defiant than I did. It was that hair.

Standing nose to nose during an argument used to make us laugh, but I wasn't in a laughing mood. (Well, actually I *was*, but this was not the time. I needed to look like I meant business.) So I turned up my nose and dropped this on her:

"It's obvious the fat cats at Herbal Excellence want to sell shampoo to a hair type that happens to be *mine*. But what I don't understand is why you entered *yours*."

Mavis sat down in front of the dreaded mirror. "Let me lay it out for you. If Herbal Excellence chooses me, then that proves they are not biased. But if they choose a girl with hair like yours, what does that say about them?"

"It says they-are-not-trying-to-sell-shampoo-to-people-wearing-Afros."

That's when Mavis put the vanity session on hold and gave me her full attention.

"Listen, Sherlock, I'm trying to school you on the haps here," she said, sounding a bit more serious than in our usual conversations. "Herbal Excellence is *goin' down*. Unless they choose me, they are anti-feminist pigs and deserve to feel the full weight of a mass boycott. I'll get a petition going and then ask all the kids at school to sign it and…"

Was my twin sister off her rocker, or was I hearing things? Mavis Marconi—the newfangled activist—wanted to take down a corporation over a hairstyle. Who was going to believe that? She was no more a victim of discrimination than a D-average student who couldn't get into Princeton.

The main reason I didn't understand all the activist attitude was that Mavis was more the artsy-craftsy type. When I overheard her phone conversation with 'the people,' she was in the basement tie-dyeing every T-shirt in our closet that didn't have a symbol smacked on it. She also made earrings, crocheted purses, and all that stuff. Ever seen a militant in macrame?

"Mavis," I said again in the calmest voice I could manage.

"It's a free country. Just because you can't get any play from a shampoo maker is not exactly grounds for a boycott. *Be for real.*"

She returned her face to the mirror. "When we get there, and they choose *your* hair over mine, then we'll see who's crazy. Now get to *that*."

I would have gladly continued this debate of duplicates, but it was just about time for our favorite radio show. If not for that, I would have given her the third degree right then and there. But I wasn't about to miss the only hour of decent entertainment I could get in this house on any day of the week. We only had one TV, and you *know* who had first dibs on that. The only time we had access to the set was Saturday morning and only until Mama woke up and made us turn off the cartoons. In one month we'd missed Super Friends three times because Mama decided to get up early.

So Mavis and I buried the hatchet for the next sixty minutes while we listened to the crackly, barely receptive station broadcast from somewhere south of Aliquippa— WPPT-FM. The radio sat on the nightstand between our beds, along with our pink Princess phone, a lamp, and my favorite school picture of Julius Barron taped to the shade. Mavis hates that I put my future boyfriend there, but I just can't go to sleep without blowing him a kiss every night. Besides, he's the finest boy in school and not an activist like his brother Gerald, who happens to be crazy about Mavis. Trouble is, he is in love alone since Mavis won't give him the time of day.

Anyway, we always turn out the lights and open the window shade so we can listen to Barry White by moonlight.

When the lights went out, I rolled my head toward Mavis and said, "Don't you just love being twins?"

And she said, "Ask me in an hour."

———

So there we were. Identical siblings with unidentical hair, courtesy of a Black mother and an Italian father, freezing our fannies off in Washington Square. Why? Because we're *twins*.

"Call me crazy," I said. "But it seems to me that proving discrimination would be easier if the sister was *not* a twin, did *not* have straight hair, and stood at the *front* of the line with a *sign*. Isn't that what real protesters do?"

For the second time she pulled down her arm, which needed to stay down considering none of 'the people' had shown up.

"Just chill out and wait. You'll see."

I shook my head at that pathetic response and said to myself. "We'll see, alright."

I turned my attention to the crowd, searching out Stephanie and Cynthia—the other Jewels who planned to enter the contest with me. Stephanie's blonde bangs made her easy to spot; they fell over her eyes and moved whenever she blinked. And that red hair of Cynthia's would stand out in any crowd.

As we got closer to the building, I figured I may as well read the piece of paper they passed out with the tickets. That's when I noticed we'd just made the age cutoff:

Welcome to the Herbal Excellence Model Search Audition
Girls ages 13 to 18 are eligible
Long, straight hair is preferable, but short, straight hair is acceptable
Your photo will be collected at check-in.
Good luck!

No sooner was I about to point out to Mavis the straight-haired part of the instructions than who walked up looking like mini militants? You guessed it, 'the people.' And not just the people, but the people leader, Gerald. Yep, the baby brother of my dream date.

"Mavis, my sister in the struggle, sorry we're late," he said, grabbing my sister's hand in a Black Power handshake. He wore a dashiki over his turtleneck and blue jeans.

"You know we wouldn't miss your activism debut, my sista," said one of the female 'people.' She had the nerve to raise her fist and then throw the peace sign. Her gold medallion glistened in the sun.

Mavis was all excited, jumping up and down like a kid. "I got this, I got this," was all she said.

"And how is the twin sister of our beloved Mavis?" Gerald said to me.

"Cold," I replied, turning the other way. I had no intention of getting pulled into a discussion about something I was dead set against. Instead, I turned my attention to a much more worthy cause: searching the square for Julius. I'd hope he'd come so he could see me get picked, which would rack up my cool points with him.

"Seems Miss Lady is upset about something," Gerald said to the back of my head.

"Oh, leave her alone," Mavis coaxed. "She's not on the same page as we are."

"You got that right," I said, swinging around to face them. "Not only am I not on the same page, um about to *book*." Mavis pulled me back in line and whispered her desperation into my ear. "Please don't go, Camille. I need you."

Yep, you guessed it. I stayed. For my *twin*. As for 'the people,' I folded my arms in defiance and ignored them for the rest of the conversation.

It took another 20 minutes before we reached the first double doors of the former furniture store on Washington Street. We were barely inside, but at least we could feel some heat. The people didn't stick around for the finish, which was just as I suspected. I could see them in the window of the Coney Island diner sipping hot cocoa. Wish I was.

And then I noticed something else.

"Mavis, look," I said, pointing to the front of the line that was now about seven girls deep. "They're splitting off up there."

We watched as the Herbal Excellence person used the end of her pencil to point girls either left or right.

"Look, they sent Stephanie to the left. That must mean something good," I said, hopeful.

That's when I felt Mavis grab my hand.

She always does that when we're facing some kind of trouble and she can't bear to find out what it is.

Three more girls to go before that pencil would be directed at us.

"Don't worry," I said. "Maybe if we keep holding hands, they'll send us together."

I said it, but I didn't believe it. At least it made Mavis lighten up on her grip. I could feel the circulation in my fingers coming back.

One more girl to go.

"Name?"

"Hazel Smith"

"Photo?"

The girl nervously handed it over.

Then it happened. Up went the pencil, and she was sent to the left. After witnessing a few girls sent in that direction, I figured left must surely be for winners, and Stephanie is as good as chosen. All of the girls sent left had really nice hair.

Then it was our turn. I stepped in front of Mavis and took her number, 82. That way, she could see it wasn't as bad as all that.

"Name?"

"Camille Marconi."

"Photo?"

"Uh, I had it right here," I said, looking up at the impatient woman while I feverishly dug through my suede purse. At first, I couldn't feel it, fingering through all the Doublemint wrappers, flavored lip gloss, and bobby pins. So I checked the pockets of my cords and my blue jean jacket. Finally, I fished it out. It was way down at the bottom of my purse amongst all that junk.

"Here it is."

She looked at my picture, and again, up went the pencil. This time it pointed to the right.

At first, I was ticked off because *I* am Camille Marconi, the one with the locks that will knock off your socks—the cool jewel who's nobody's fool. How could they send *me* to the right? In spite of how much I'd hated coming to this thing and how long I had stood out in the cold, I had actually expected to be the *chosen* one. I'd never won a contest. *Ever.* Not even a call-in radio show. I would always dial the last number just a little bit too late. Of course, I didn't make enough of those calls to develop a system or anything, but I'd *personally* shown up to this joint, and they had the nerve to deny me my one chance to win?

In a huff, I immediately looked back to see where Mavis was, and sure enough, the pencil went up, and she was sent left.

My sister, the *Afro-wearing* twin. How could that happen when Herbal Excellence never, and I mean ever, uses Afros in their ads? While my mouth hung open on the right, Mavis kept waving at me from the left.

Well, one thing was for sure: I wouldn't have to worry about my sister protesting Herbal Excellence. But something still bugged me: why did they choose *her*?

CHAPTER 2

Marvin Gaye once said, 'Only believe half of what you see,' and it's true because it turned out that at the audition, the right was *really* right and the left was for losers. I immediately thought of Stephanie, who also went left. The Jewels would never hear the end of it at school next week.

After all the girls were chosen, the 'right' girls and I were told 'congratulations.' I watched Mavis over on the left. Cynthia and her bright red hair were there, too. *Bummer*.

The woman with the pencil was no doubt thanking all the 'left' girls for their effort while handing out bags of beauty products.

I was right on time when I ran over there and stopped Mavis before she swung her bag at the woman.

"Mavis, what's up? Isn't this what you wanted, to lose so you could protest?"

She looked like she was going to swing the bag at me, but she calmed down; after all, we are twins.

"Yeah, yeah, let's get out of here. I've got work to do."

Yep. It was like I'd been saying all along: Herbal

Excellence never, and I mean ever, used Afros in their ads, so they invited me and my straight hair to the second audition along with about 50 other straight-haired girls.

I knew I didn't have a shot—most of the girls they picked in Round One had baby-fine hair. Perfectly smooth, perfectly shiny, and perfectly perfect. It was a sight to behold because Stephanie and Cynthia were a shoo-in, and they didn't get picked.

Now *I* was going to the second audition. Of course, I did feel bad for Mavis. We stood in that line for hours only to have them tell her she didn't make it.

When we got home, I made a pit stop in the kitchen. Mama was in there rustling through cabinets and pulling out pots for dinner. I stayed to talk to her while Mavis rushed upstairs.

My eyes followed her while I popped peanuts into my mouth from the candy dish on the table.

"So how did it go?" While Mama opened some cans of green beans, she kept her eyes on me, a smirk of a smile on her face.

"I got picked," then a twinge of guilt made me lower my eyes, "but Mavis didn't." I popped another peanut. "And she had the nerve to get mad about it, too. Weird."

Mama put down the can opener, crossed her arms, and glared.

"What?"

She went back to her can opener. "Honestly, Camille, you can't be that blind."

I stopped in mid-pop. "What's that supposed to mean?"

She lowered her eyes, and that smile crept back onto her face. "Mavis is not just your twin, Camille; she's a girl. A young girl just like you—" She chuckled. "Well, not *just* like you, but she has feelings."

I couldn't be sure, but my rolled lip and lowered lids must've convinced Mama that I wasn't buying it.

She pushed the cans aside and leaned toward me. "If one of your little friends told you she didn't want to win a beauty contest, would you believe her? —"

I had to think on that; I knew how much Stephanie wanted to win, and Cynthia, she'll be dogging the contest 'til the cows come home. She went left, too. The best answer I could come up with was, "But they're not like Mavis—"

"They're girls, and Mavis is a girl. No matter what "cause" she's fighting for, Camille, your sister still has feelings. Losing that contest was a rejection, whether it was real or imagined, and nobody wants to be rejected."

Mama got up to put a saucepan on the stove, and in a curious voice, she asked, "How did you feel when you found out you were a contestant?

She turned to me for an answer, but I couldn't respond. Something made my eyes lower again, so I popped another peanut.

"I thought so," she said, with her back to me.

Unlike Daddy, who always had some lesson to teach, Mama only dished it out on a need-to-know basis.

So when I got upstairs, I told Mavis I wasn't going to go through with it. But instead of agreeing to give up her plan, Mavis concocted this ridiculous little scheme for us *both* to go to the second audition so she could try to convince the company to create two ads: one for Afros and one for straight hair. If I'd let her go through with it, we'd get our faces crushed, and I'd lose my chance to show Julius that I was a winner and make the Cool Jewels proud of me.

"I'll stand right beside you," she said with wicked delight. "And on cue, we both will say, 'afro or straight, Herbal Excellence is great!'

I know. Stupid, right? And boy did I want to tell her that, but nope. You know why? Because we're twins.

The day of the audition, there I was, sitting in the backseat of Mama's Gremlin, complete with lipstick, a ton of blush, and an uneasy feeling in my gut. Good thing I remembered to slip that picture of Julius into my purse. I needed a confidence booster right about now.

As the Gremlin puttered, Mavis muttered, still determined to go through with her plan. "And if they don't agree, they'll see how Mavis Marconi gets down."

And, when translated, that meant yours truly would *somehow* get the short end of the stick. It was the law of Mavis averages.

The second audition was on the other side of town; that's why we asked Mama to drive us. Despite the ridiculousness of this scheme, she agreed to put her soap operas on hold to take us to Round Two. "If it's that important to you, we'll go." Then through a smile she said, "I'd like to see what happens myself. Times are changing, and companies that sell to Black folk should celebrate all our styles." You should have seen Mavis' face after that speech. I couldn't tell her nothin'.

I wish Mama hadn't decided to take this school bus-yellow car instead of Daddy's new Buick Elektra 225. When the Gremlin came out, all the kids laughed over its funny shape. It got so bad that anytime we missed the bus, we had Mama drop us a block away so no one would see us getting out of it. We told her there was a new rule: no cars in front of the school—for safety reasons. She never questioned it.

When we rolled up on the joint, Mavis jumped out, turned to me, and repeated her instructions.

"Soon as they call your name, we'll both stand tall and proud, then walk right up and let them know we're not going to stand for their unfair treatment. We are proud African queens and—"

"All right already. I got it," I said, adjusting my suede mini skirt. Sitting in that sauna-with-a-sunroof always made my dresses ride up. I'd hoped my lack of enthusiasm would change my sister's mind. It didn't; Mama went off to park, while we went off to get embarrassed.

The Herbal Excellence people were set up in a temporary building again. As I was checking out the place, I imagined that finding locations for photo shoots and stuff like that might be fun. Mavis would be great at that. In fact, she could be my personal photographer (especially since she wasn't going to be in any shampoo commercial).

We were taken to a big office with slick decorations, and all their folks were dressed to the nines. One of the guys wore an argyle sweater, wide-wale corduroys, and Earth shoes. A woman was sporting those new elephant bell-bottoms over a beige popcorn bodysuit. I loved bodysuits because you never had to tuck your shirt inside your pants, and the popcorn puffs all over it were out of sight. The pant legs were so wide they almost covered her platforms. That outfit was BAD.

So my suede skirt and matching tank top fit right in. Mavis wore her *hot* hot pants, the ones with the hand she sewed on the butt, which I thought was so tacky, and I told her so. You think she cared?

Model material she is not.

We found a seat with the other girls and waited for *my* turn. A few of them scoped us out with their mouths open. What made them think that twins couldn't be in a commercial? (I mean, *we* won't be, but you know what I'm saying).

When the Herbal Excellence spokesperson came out to greet us, I grabbed Mavis' hand. Not because I was nervous, but because she couldn't be trusted. Both Mama and I were afraid that if she was let loose in this place, she might go off on them, and we'd end up on the six o'clock news.

"Camille Marconi."

Hearing my name gave me the willies. This was finally my chance to be the kind of girl Julius would be proud to have on his arm. I stood tall (if not proud) and walked right over to the woman with the clipboard in her hand. The same woman who had the magical 'pencil' wand.

When Mavis jumped up and stood beside me, the woman looked at my photo and raised a brow.

"You're not Camille Marconi?"

"I *know* that," Mavis said.

"Well," said the woman, still giving off that suspicious look, "I recall telling *Camille* Marconi to come back today. I also recall telling *you* that we are not featuring Afros in this commercial. I am sorry, but that's just the way it is."

She said this in an 'I-don't-have-time-for-games' tone, so I figured Mavis' idea was out in the cold, but little did I know she was just warming up.

"I am *Mavis* Marconi, and I know you didn't expect to see me or my Afro, but—"

"Come on, Mavis," I said, holding tight to her hand. "Maybe you should go see what's keeping Mama."

But Mavis was on a roll.

"… did you ever consider doing *two* commercials?" She continued while wringing her hand free. "… one showing a girl wearing a 'fro in that tulip garden and another showing a girl with straight hair?"

The woman probably thought we were two of the craziest kids she'd ever seen. With all the eyes on our tug-of-war, we were more like clowns.

"No, Miss Marconi," she replied, "but thank you for your time, and have a nice day."

"Fine," Mavis said, raising the peace sign on her way out. "You'll be hearing from me."

I stood there looking like a dunce and feeling like a fool, and the only thing I could say was, "I'm still a finalist, right?"

———

WHEN THE AUDITION was over and I got to the car, Mavis and I locked eyes. She knew before I opened my mouth that I made the cut, and she wasn't having ANY of it.

"Let's forget it, Mavis," I said, securing her seat belt nice and tight. "Can't you just be happy for me?"

"Happy? That my sister is about to be exploited by a racist hair company and she's going along with it? Oh, trust me. You ain't seen nothin' yet."

I sank into the backseat and let her rant. What could I do? She spoiled the whole thing to the point that I couldn't even enjoy the moment. *My* moment. I won something. Something that would impress Julius. And what did she do? Dump on it.

To be completely honest, Mavis wasn't always this high-strung, but when she did feel challenged, you couldn't change her mind, which worried me, because I already knew her next move: protest.

"So how do you suppose you're going to get back at a big corporation, Mavis? You can't prove they've done anything wrong."

She glared at me like I was the Devil himself. "*You* are what's wrong. As long as you play into their hands by going along with this mess, you're puttin' down your own brothers and sisters."

"How you figure that?"

"You know how," she said, pointing her finger in my face. "We may be half Italian, but we're also half Black. Doesn't that mean anything to you?"

"Excuse me?" I hated it when Mavis questioned my

loyalties. "For your information, I'm just as Black as you and just as *Italian*, so take a chill pill."

"That's enough, both of you," Mama scolded the rearview mirror. "I've told you about fighting over race, in this car or anywhere else."

Mavis kept her trap shut for the rest of the ride home. In fact, nobody said nothing, which was just the way I liked it. The problem was the minute we hit the door, "nothing" wouldn't be the last thing I heard.

CHAPTER 3

t wasn't until I had bathed, brushed, and crawled into bed that Mavis decided to make herself clear regarding her planned protest of Herbal Excellence. By then she'd calmed all the way down, which meant she was about to get dangerous.

"Can't you see, Camille? We have a chance to strike a blow for Black women everywhere. Heck, maybe even other women, too. Have you seen any shampoo commercials featuring Asian women or even Indian women?"

"No," I said, with my back against the headboard, and if I had to listen to much more of this nonsense, I'd be banging my head against it. But I had to be calm, like my girls at school. We chose the name Cool Jewels because we knew how to keep it together no matter what the weather. So I took a deep breath, retaped my picture of Julius to the lampshade, and tried to ignore her.

"If I can organize this protest," she continued, "I'd be standing up for women everywhere; you know what I'm saying?"

Frankly, I had no idea what she was saying. I could

sympathize if she was uptight because Herbal Excellence was making a mockery of the Afro, because that would've been an affront to half our race, but this was nothing like that. Personally, I thought she was just jealous, but did I say that to my twin? No way, Jose.

I mean, is it really such a big deal if Herbal Excellence wants to cater to the straight and silky?

Before I could ask that question, Mavis gave me an answer.

"Don't you get it? We women are liberated in everything, including the style of our hair. If we can force them to create shampoo for both nappy and straight hair, they'd make more money and we'd have more choices. Humph. They'll either get it together or get gangstered."

She pulled the covers over her knees and leaned back on her pillow like she'd just finished a speech, but before she started in with 'I have a dream,' the sequel, I turned over and pretended *I* was dreaming. In my opinion, that Afro was not only on her head, it was going *to* her head. It was up to me to save my sister from herself and save the fat cats at Herbal Excellence from this Gloria Steinem stand-in. In such times of sudden stress, I did what Daddy always did when he faced an especially difficult obstacle: write to Dear Addy.

So first thing the next morning I took my wickedly writerly self to my desk and wrote a letter:

Dear Addy Van Austen,

I'm 13 and a half. I am also a twin. But lately she is not acting very twinly, and that is why I am writing to you. My sister is trying to start a riot by protesting the fact that Herbal Excellence does not make shampoo for Afros. On top of that, they chose me to be a finalist in their upcoming commercial, and she won't even give me support. What do I do?

Sincerely,

Taunted Twin

In case Mrs. Van Austen decided to immortalize me in print, I didn't use my real name. Most people who wrote Dear Addy didn't. Daddy never had.

I stuffed the letter into an envelope and licked my eight-cent stamp to seal the deal. I was taking it to the mailbox when Mavis came running outside.

"I hope that letter is not to Herbal Excellence, Camille, because if it is, and you ruin this protest, I will never speak to you again." She kept trying to peek over the envelope I was now holding close to my chest.

"Mavis, I wouldn't dare write those fat cats a letter and expose your little conspiracy. Then I wouldn't have the pleasure of seeing the whole thing blow up in your face in front of the kids at school, your teachers, and Mama. Sorry, but I'm just keeping it real."

I quickly threw the letter into the mailbox, closed the metal door, and raised the red flag. I hoped that my hugging the mailbox wasn't raising any other red flags.

"Honestly, Camille, why this contest means so much to you and that stringy hair of yours, I'll never know. But you can bet your last money that when this protest puts you *out* of the spotlight, you'll be thanking me."

The only thing I was thankful for was seeing her walk away.

Before we left for school, I snatched the letter out of the box and asked Mama to mail it when she went to work. No sense taking any chances.

When we boarded the school bus, Mavis pulled a yellow notepad out of the pukey green backpack she got from the Army/Navy store. No girls with class carried a military-style backpack to school. None. Mavis's nod to the struggle somehow meant she had to represent. But Mavis loves to

dress, so the bag was as far as *that* went. No red, black, or
green has graced our closet so far (and I'm keeping my
fingers crossed).

By the time we got to first-period study hall, I discovered
something else Mavis had in her backpack: about ten
handwritten notes on index cards, in the fancy script my
sister loved:

Fight the Man!!
Support Women's Rights!!
Don't Buy Herbal Excellence Shampoo!!

My sister. My *twin* sister was becoming a full-fledged
fanatic. How did she turn into such a pig-headed publicity
hound?

"The world needs to know about discrimination wherever
it is," she said to me as she stuck her personal agenda onto
anything that didn't repel masking tape. "By the time I'm
through with Herbal Excellence, they'll think twice before
messing with Mavis Marconi."

"A boycott is a big deal, Mavis," I said. "The ones I've
seen on TV can last a long time, and sometimes they don't
even work."

Of course, she and her plan to stick it to the man were
already in motion, so, not knowing what the endgame would
be to her hair-raising high jinks, I concluded that the only
way to get Mavis to cease and desist was to *pretend* to assist.
"Why don't you give me the rest of those, and I'll get them
put up?" I said.

Mavis stopped for a moment to check me. Twins always
know what twins really mean, even if they say something
they don't really mean.

"Oh, no, you don't. Until you show me you're completely

on board, I don't trust you as far as I can see you. Meet you at lunch?"

"Sure," I said. When she was out of sight, I pulled the index card off my locker door and threw it in the first trashcan I found.

Bon Voyage, fancy script.

CHAPTER 4

George Washington Junior High is not very special, just your typical institute of high enough learning. It has brick on the outside, boredom on the inside, and lots of drama in between.

I kept it moving so I wouldn't be late, styling and profiling in my pink linen baby doll shirt and matching gauchos. I was cooler than cold, which made me wonder why none of "the people" had an eye for what was fly. Most of them strutted around in the same three shades: red, black, and green—the 'official' colors of the Motherland. Of course, no one at school was more into those colors than Gerald. After elementary school, I was convinced that Mavis had gone into activism overdrive, but compared to Gerald, she was a late bloomer. The three of us had gone to the same school until 3rd grade, when Gerald's family moved to Africa. They came back last year, and now Gerald and Mavis were in the same history class. Ever since they got reacquainted, he'd turned her on to a lot of the causes she held dear. I could still remember our first day of junior high when we caught the bus home. She was so excited about all his adventures she could hardly take a breath.

"He's been on a safari in the Congo and rode a camel in Sudan. He's been overseas, Camille." She swooned. "You know how super cool that is?"

"Living in Africa sounds kind of scary to me," I said. "All those natives running around with spears, all those wild animals. No thanks. I'll take the good old U.S. of A. any day."

Mavis giggled, "You watch too many Tarzan movies. Africa is not like that anymore. Gerald told me that most of the countries are run completely by Black people. They've got their own businesses and schools and their very own government."

"That's not what I heard," I said. "I watch the news with Mama sometimes, and all they say is how bad it is for Blacks in South Africa. The people on the screen didn't look too happy, either. Guess Gerald didn't live there."

"Why do you always have to take something good and turn it around? He was just dropping some knowledge on me about how free they—well, some of them—are. Good grief, Charlie Brown."

Mavis turned to face the seat in front of us and stuck out the usual bottom lip.

"So do you like him or something?" I had to ask because Mavis had never talked about anyone like that before.

"Gerald? No. Why can't girls just be friends with boys anyway?"

"I guess it's possible, but in junior high, when a girl talks like you're talking, it's usually a sign."

"Oh, does that go for you and *Julius* too?" She shot back, throwing me off guard. But I recovered quick.

"Unlike Gerald, Julius is not splashing all over *me* like Niagara Falls—"

"But you *wish* he was." My sister recovers quick, too. The upturned corner of her lip caused me to lean back in my seat;

after all, she was right. And *that* was the last time she shared anything with me about Gerald.

But I knew of what I spoke. Ever since the first grade, Gerald had eyes for Mavis. She never noticed it, but I did. We'd be in the schoolyard playing jacks, jumping rope, or just talking, and there was Gerald, his heart hanging onto the chain-link fence of love. Or I'd see him standing in the hallway, hoping Mavis would honor him with a glance or a smile or our phone number. But on Mavis's measuring tape of potential men, Gerald was an eighth of an inch.

'Can I have a chance?' The boys would say to girls they wanted to date. Those words never came out of Gerald's mouth. He was only good for a "right on" here or a "power to the people" there. The ways of love were not his thing.

Anyway, getting back to my story, once class let out, I was headed toward the cafeteria to get with the Jewels when Gerald slid into lockstep with me. He was no doubt trying to get some tips to use on Mavis.

Gerald really was a nice-looking dude. Not as cute as his brother, of course, but with a few upgrades his cool factor could rise to higher heights. For one thing, all that red, black, and green had to go. I often wondered if he had any hair left under that crocheted cap he always wore.

"Come on, Camille. What can I do to get her to like me?" he asked.

"She does like you," I said, though I knew what he really meant. I just wanted to hear him say it. "She talks about your life in Africa all the time—"

"Is that all?"

"OK, Gerald. For starters, be cool. Maybe she'd give you some play if you acted more like a man and not a militant."

"See, that's where you're wrong, Camille. Mavis and I are cut from the same dashiki. We appreciate the Motherland and the struggle. That's what makes us so perfect for each other. I wouldn't expect you to understand."

"And what's that supposed to mean?"

He shrugged and walked backward down the hall. If he'd hung around long enough, I could have ragged on that stupid cap, but I was already late for lunch, and Mavis hated to eat alone.

One thing I had to admit about Mavis: she really got down in the coordination category. She could make that 'fro match anything. She'd always come into the lunchroom looking like she knew all eyes were on her. Almost like she counted on them to co-sign her style. I noticed kids checking out her blue jean gauchos, dangling feather earrings dyed turquoise green, and matching tie-dyed T-shirt. Not my taste, but it worked for her.

I regretted the day I bought her that box of Rit, though, because Mavis didn't rinse out the washer after she was done dyeing those T-shirts. Mama was madder than a wet hen when she pulled out her white sheets. They looked like they'd come from some rock star's bed.

At lunch, I couldn't resist telling Mavis about my encounter with Gerald. How he kept pumping me for information about her 'perfect man.' Maybe I could convince her that he was at least worth considering, even if "weak rap" wasn't on her list of boyfriend requirements. Besides, they were tit for tat on all things radical, so if she would give the boy a chance, it might get me in with Julius.

"Guess who was hounding me out in the hallway?" I said to her.

"Not Gerald again?"

"None other. He tries so hard, Mavis. Why don't you go ahead and give him a chance?"

"Gerald? I mean, I truly love his commitment to the

struggle, but I'm not sure that I like him like that. Maybe if he had a little more hair—"

"You can't even see his hair. Maybe if he had a little more rap."

"That's not fair, and you know it. Not every boy can be Julius Barron."

"Gimme some skin on that," I said, standing with my palm raised.

"Sit down, Camille. You look silly."

Instead, I made my way to the Jewels, who were sitting two tables away and having a deep discussion about the new dry shampoo that just came out.

"It's called Psssst!," Stephanie said, her eyes blinking beneath those perfectly blonde bangs. "And it's only $1.99, so we must get some this weekend."

If anyone knew the latest this or that, it was Stephanie. She kept all of us up-to-date on hairstyles, hair products, and lipstick. When the pot o' gloss came out, the Cool Jewels were the first girls to wear it, and we looked good, too, except when we ate our sandwiches, because that gloss stuck to bread like glue.

"Why did they give it such a funny name? Doesn't sound very cool to me," said Cynthia.

She's the critic of the group. She makes sure we always look fly, and if even a hair is out of place, Cynthia lets us know it. Cynthia and Stephanie are white, not mixed like me. In fact, I'm the only one in the group. But then, none of the other black girls have straight hair like ours, and only straight-haired girls are allowed in.

When I rolled up, the conversation stopped. And a strange silence rested on each one of them. I hesitated before sitting down, until Stephanie threw her arms around me.

"You did it," she squealed. "You put us on the map."

I mustered a nervous smile as each Jewel came over to congratulate me.

"You know what this means, don't you," Cynthia said with a sly look on her face. "We have to go shopping."

"Yes," said Stephanie. "Your hair has to be perfect for the audition—"

"Look who just walked in." Stephanie nudged me to turn around.

It was Julius. Great googly moogly! His smooth, dark skin and almost-deep voice could turn any girl into a silly love slave.

He was in the lunch line with his fine self.

"I gotta go," I said and made my way back to Mavis. The last thing I wanted was for Julius to think we were silly.

I remembered the first time I noticed him. I was only 9, and he was 11. I guess I was as bad as Gerald in those days because I'd stop playing jacks to watch Julius shoot hoops on the playground. And I LOVED Jacks. I even convinced the principal to put some greasy surfaces on the concrete planters where we played so we could scoop up our jacks without scratching our palms. Since I was willing to allow Julius to divert my attention from my most favorite game, I knew that I REALLY liked him.

But I was just one of many girls swooning over his good looks, his height, and his beautiful white teeth. Julius was the kind of guy who showed complete class. I remembered the day he walked by when Mavis and I were playing hopscotch.

"Hi," was all he said to us, flashing those pearly whites.

"Hi, Julius," I said with a lump in my throat.

"Come on, Camille, it's your turn," Mavis complained. But I didn't even hear her. I couldn't take my eyes off those teeth.

That's when he did the most wonderful thing: he winked at me, and my heart melted all over the concrete. I stood there like a statue until he walked away. He kept turning around, waving at me.

"Wake up, Camille," Mavis had said, trying to return my attention to hopscotch. "He's just a boy."

Ha, that's where she was wrong. Julius was not just a boy. He was a prince. Those were the days. And I could finally have my chance to be his princess as soon as I won that contest.

Anyway, at my sister's bidding, I sat down and opened my peanut butter sandwich from home and put my chips next to it on a napkin, being careful not to spill anything on my pink outfit. I liked all my stuff to be in order. "Gerald did do something today that made me wonder about him," I said.

"Did he try to hit on you?"

"No, dummy, he likes 'em militant, remember? Anyway, he didn't come out and say what he meant, but I got the message." Then I took my hand, pulled up a lock of my hair, and let it drop. "He practically cracked on me for not living up to his image of the Beautiful Black Woman."

All she did was grunt. Like she was in full agreement. I put down my chips and picked up my pride.

"I don't care what you or Gerald think. Just because somebody wears an Afro doesn't *automatically* make them Black. White kids wear them, too. You and I are mixed, remember? Which *means that we are not completely Black.*"

My teeth tore into my peanut butter sandwich while my demeanor dared her to devise a comeback.

Mavis leaned back in her plastic chair like she was contemplating a move. I kept right on chomping. Then she did the last thing I would have expected. She took her lunch, her purse, and her attitude and left. I would have called her out, but all that peanut butter had my lips on lockdown. She never looked back. That's when I knew the battle of the century was about to begin.

CHAPTER 5

J ust when I thought things couldn't get any worse, they
did. Like the day I got called back to Herbal Excellence
for another audition. Yep. I officially became a finalist,
and Mavis officially became my enemy. On the other hand,
the Jewels were ecstatic. At least somebody was supporting
me.

"Come on, Mavis, if you don't get up right now, we're
going to be late." I stood at the end of the bed, reached under
the covers for both her ankles, and pulled, but she kicked me
away.

"I'm not going," she said, and faked a cough. "I'm sick."

I straightened my stance, hands on hips, and proceeded to
talk some sense into her.

"Isn't it against the rules of radicalism to let a white
shampoo company come between you and your kin? Isn't
that why they made Afro Sheen?"

She sat up in bed and crossed her arms. "Haven't you ever
heard of integration?"

I raised a doubting eyebrow at her sudden recovery.

"You're just being stubborn—"

"And you're not?"

I felt heat in my cheeks, but my mouth wouldn't open. She smirked and turned her face to the pillow.

"Camille! Mavis! Let's go."

"Coming, Mama." I said as I turned on my heel and left my unsupportive sister. I had no plans to let her ruin my only chance at stardom.

Downstairs, I grabbed my coat and headed for the door.

"Where's Mavis?" Mama looked toward the stairs like she expected to see my sister.

"She's in bed," I hollered from the front door. "And she can rot there for all I care."

Mama was silent in the car, which told me she was not happy about the fact that Mavis and I were feuding, but if she had anything to say to *me* about it, she never did. What *could* she say? Here I was facing the chance of a lifetime to make our family proud and famous, and all Mavis could do was sulk. I figured Mama agreed with me, so I spent the rest of the ride in my head, rehearsing my acceptance speech.

When we arrived, Mama drove me to the front door, put the car in park, and sat there. The car was still running.

"I'll wait for you while you park," I said, then popped out of the passenger side.

"I'm not coming in, Camille. I made an appointment with Missy for a perm. You'll do fine on your own, and I will be right here when you come out. Besides, Mama would just make you nervous."

She smiled. I sighed. Then I went inside.

This was the last audition before Herbal Excellence made a beeline out of the backwoods of Pennsylvania. They promised to send the final decision by First Class Mail to all participants.

At the door, a woman stood holding cards. As each girl entered, she handed out a card. My card had a number on it:

82. The same number I had in line that cold day on Washington Street. I took that as a sign.

The audition room was jam-packed with pretty-haired girls who wore pretty serious curls. Some in mini-dresses, others in wide-legged jeans. I wore my new purple knickers and matching polyester pullover. I knew I looked good.

Another woman directed us to sit in chairs close to a stage that had a microphone on a stand, and I wondered if that's where we would end up. In front of the footlights.

Every girl in that joint was all smiles, with the exception of one. She looked like me, like she was mixed. Most of the girls there were white. Something I never really noticed at the first audition, but when I thought back to that day, it was the same situation. Guess I was too busy watching out for my sister to notice.

"Hi," I said to her. "I'm Camille."

"I'm Lydia."

I looked around the room at the sea of happy hopefuls. "Isn't this the coolest thing? I wonder how many finalists they'll pick today?"

But my enthusiasm was lost on Lydia.

"I just want to get this over with," she said in a dry voice. "It's all such a bunch of crap."

Her attitude took me by surprise, mainly because it wasn't what I expected, and I was sure my face gave that away.

She smiled. "Yeah, you'd think I would be down with this game since my hair is straight and I'm light-skinned, but this is my mom's dream, not mine. She wants her 'little girl' to be a big star, like Lena Horne or somebody, but I'm not interested in all that. I'd rather be at home sewing cool patches on my jeans."

As she spoke, I thought about Mavis. She and this girl would get along great.

"Why wouldn't you want to win?" I asked, and I knew I sounded as shocked as I felt. "You're beautiful."

Lydia's eyes rolled to the ceiling and back. "Because it's exploitation, my sister. And I, for one, am not down with that. Look around; do you see any Afros?"

That's when *my* eyes rolled. *An activist with ash blonde hair.* But before I could respond, the woman on stage announced it was showtime.

My seat in front of the stage was a few rows behind Lydia's, which made me glad because I did not want to be a part of any protest she might've had in mind.

But when it was her turn to go on stage—which was to the right and up a few stairs—she went left and walked out of the room. She never came back.

After that, I didn't pay much attention to the other girls or what they said on stage. Even when it was my turn, the excitement I came into this joint with had been reduced by half. *Why did I let Lydia spoil my moment?*

At the mic, we had to explain why we wanted to be in the Herbal Excellence commercial, and as soon as the word 'I' came out of my mouth, the excitement returned, and I pretty much blabbed about how I was meant to be a model—for nearly 10 minutes.

In the car, Mama asked how it went.

"I think I did OK," I said, not sounding too convincing. "This girl in line ahead of me kind of threw me off my game." Mama glanced over from the driver's side like she was waiting for the rest of the story, so I told it. "She said her mom made her enter the contest. And worst of all, she feels just like Mavis does about it." I slumped against the door Daddy always said never to lean on. If I fell out today, it'd be just as well. "This anti-Herbal Excellence thing is like a disease, and everybody's got it."

Mama reached over and patted my thigh. "I know you've

got your heart set on winning this contest, Camille, but you have to admit what they're doing does sound like discrimination."

"It's just shampoo, Mama. *Shampoo.*"

She gave me one of those motherly smiles that said she thought I was wrong but didn't want to discourage me. "It means more than shampoo to Mavis, honey. And a lot of other people, too."

"Fine." I said, still slumping. "Anyway, I sort of ran off at the mouth in there about how much I wanted to win, so chances are, I won't."

And I knew at least one person who would be very happy to hear that.

CHAPTER 6

I dropped my purse in a kitchen chair and my rump in the one next to it. I couldn't stop thinking about Lydia and the possibility of losing my spot in the limelight. The two thoughts were like fire and water, and I couldn't get them to agree. I went to the fridge to get a glass of milk and to the cupboard for some graham crackers. I gulped, munched, and mulled over the whole situation.

Was it wrong that I wanted this so badly?

For the life of me, I still didn't get the big deal. At least Herbal Excellence was honest, not pandering to Black Power. You'd think that would mean *something* to Mavis.

I wiped my mouth with my forearm and immediately regretted it. My new polyester pullover was now stained with milky cinnamon and sugar.

I took what was left of my snack to our room. When I got there, Mavis was working on another hook rug creation. She looked up and waited for me to break the news. I set my milk and crackers on the nightstand between us.

"I don't know how I did. But you don't care anyway." I flopped backward onto my twin bed and stayed there.

Mavis hooked another row, then handed me this line:

"I'm not gonna fight with you if that's what you want. But I will say this: if you are not down with the program and Julius finds that out, he'll never look at you as a girlfriend or any other kind of friend. He's not into airheads—"

That was it. I jumped from the bed, grabbed the first object in sight, and slung it in her direction. Mavis found herself and her hook rug covered in milk.

"What is your *problem*?" She ran to the bathroom, no doubt for a towel. I watched the tiny threads of yarn float in little white pools on her bed.

That's when Mama hollered from her room. "Whatever you two are doing. Don't make me come in there."

Mavis pointed toward Mama's voice and nodded. "When I tell her what you did, you're gonna get it." She sopped up the spots and crawled back onto the bed. I switched on the radio, and for the next few hours I listened and she hooked.

I was in another world that night, straining to hear Marvin Gaye belt out "Distant Lover." I needed a mood setter, and Marvin always did the trick. I didn't care what Mavis said about Julius. She didn't even know him. So I sat back and let the music saturate my senses, wondering if my gift was still saturating her sheets.

The crackly reception from the radio station made the words even more difficult to decipher. But no matter how faint it sounded, it was the closest thing to wonderful in my whole life. That was until the princess phone on our nightstand rang. We never picked up when Mama was at home, and when she didn't call our names, I knew it wasn't for us. Then Mama came storming through our bedroom door with the big news.

"Mavis. Camille. Your daddy's on the phone. He's back. Back in the United States."

Mama's words fell all over themselves, making her sound

like Porky Pig. She didn't even bother to turn on the light. Just swung open the door and started screeching.

We got up and ran behind her. She practically flew to the downstairs telephone.

"Here, here they are, dear," Mama said, pushing the receiver toward the first hand she saw.

Mavis grabbed it. "Hi, Daddy. Where are you?"

I watched Mama pace the floor. She seemed to be laughing and crying at the same time. She must have been really nervous because she kept running her fingers through her hair even though she'd just had it done.

Mama never messes with her hair on salon day.

"Okay, Daddy. Camille is right here."

"Are you girls behaving for your mama?" Daddy asked.

"Uh, of course, Daddy, we're being your little angels," I said, giving Mama a wide but nervous smile. She closed her eyes and shook her head.

"I love you, too, Daddy. Here's Mama." As soon as I handed over the phone, I tried to get away, but Mama was too quick. She held the phone with one hand and grabbed the back of my long johns with the other. I always wore them to bed in the winter. It gets really cold in PA. Had it not been for the elastic band, I could have been clean to the kitchen and in record time.

Funny thing, Mama just kept talking to Daddy as if I wasn't there. But she never let go of my long johns. Mavis was at the top of the stairs now, looking down and laughing.

"I love you, too, dear. Uh huh. Okay. Love you more. Bye."

Mama gently rested the receiver back on the cradle of the phone, still holding tight to my pajamas.

"Mavis," she called to the upstairs. "Get down here right now."

When Mavis stood before us, Mama finally let me go. I felt

my long johns sag. So did my heart. They'd be no good from then on.

"Come on, let's go upstairs," Mama said, eyeing us like a detective. "One of you better start talking or else."

I didn't want to find out what the "else" was, and I've never, ever had to find out before, because somebody always started talking. So I waited for Mavis. And waited. And waited.

"Okay," Mama said, "then I guess you want to face the consequences—"

"No, Mama, it was Mavisy," I blurted. "She made me throw that milk."

"Made you?" Mama said, eyes as wide as saucers.

I prepared my behind for the belt, knowing my sister would blame it all on me.

"Would this have something to do with that Herbal Excellence audition?" asked Mama.

Mavis yelled in my face, "You're so prejudiced you can't even see it."

"Am not."

"Are too."

"Quiet, both of you. What has gotten into you two? If this contest is going to cause all this foolishness, I think you need to forget the whole thing."

"No, Mama. I have to stay in the contest—"

"Tell her why, Camille?" Mavis raised an eyebrow like she dared me to do it. "Go on, tell her."

Mama crossed her arms and waited. I didn't know what to say.

"Well, you can tell me now, or you can explain it to your father when he gets home tomorrow."

I marched right out of the room and headed for Mama's. I couldn't talk in front of Mavis—she was already biased. I had to unload on somebody who hadn't already judged me without a jury, and Mama was the only somebody around. Mavis *knew* the rule. Ever since Daddy left, we started it: if one twin went into Mama's room, it was off limits to the other. The first time one of us used it, Mavis wanted to tell Mama some personal stuff she was going through during her cycle. Not sure why I couldn't hear it, too, but she was adamant about not sharing with me. Turns out I had the same issue, but we still kept the rule on the off chance that somewhere down the road, there'd be a situation where our twinness didn't apply. This was *definitely* that situation.

Mama and Daddy's room was kinda dark. They kept the curtains closed; at least they were closed whenever I got in there. I sat in the only chair in the room and waited. Mama finally came in and shut the door, but she kept the curtains open. It was nighttime, so it didn't matter. She sat on the edge of the bed and leaned toward me. "You know your father is not going to be happy when he hears about how you two are acting. What do you have to say for yourself?"

I wondered what took Mama so long to come in. Obviously she had asked Mavis *first*, and I could just imagine how my sister explained it, blaming the whole thing on me and leaving out the part where she insulted me, so I decided to answer her question with a question.

"It depends. What did Mavis tell you?"

"Look, Camille, this feud between the two of you has got to stop. It's unhealthy. You are twins and sisters and family and—"

"But she DOES NOT CARE, Mama. She doesn't care about ME. ME. All she cares about are her stupid causes. Nothing else matters to her."

My eyes filled with tears, so I threw my palms over them. As I cried, I felt her arms wrap around me, which made me cry harder. It took about 5 minutes before I could get myself together enough to explain, and thank goodness Mavis didn't

burst in the room. I really needed to vent. "Every time she
comes up with some idea or plan or whatever, she always
expects me to support her. She doesn't ask my opinion. She
never says, 'do you want to Camille?' She just expects it.
Always. But the minute I want something or have good news
to share, she isn't interested. It's not fair, Mama. She knew I
was entering the contest, and now that I have a chance to win,
she's a downer." Mama sighed and kept silent while I
continued my rant. I knew she couldn't really solve the
problem, but it was enough that she at least listened. "I just
want her to give me the same support she always expects
from me. That's all."

"I understand," Mama said. "And it's not too much to ask.
But you can't allow the things she says make you want to
hurt her—"

"I know, I'm sorry. She just made me so mad."

"Do you remember what we taught you as little girls—"

I recalled the saying and said in a sheepish tone, "Sticks
and stones may break my bones, but words will never
hurt me."

Mama smiled and hugged me again. "That's right. So
what are you going to do from now on?"

I let out a loud breath. "I won't be violent. But what are
you gonna make *her* do?"

Mama stood. "I am going to leave that to your father. He'll
make that decision."

I closed my lids and dropped my chin in my hands.
Family court. Never looked forward to it, and neither did
Mavis. But there it was, and if that's what it took, I was down
with it.

CHAPTER 7

The day Daddy came home, Mama announced that we weren't going to Augustine's like we usually did on special occasions. Instead, the families were coming over for an indoor barbecue.

"Where is Daddy?" I asked her. He'd come in late last night, and we couldn't see him before school because Mama wanted him to rest.

"I dropped him off at Uncle Sil's for a few hours. He and Isabella were dying to see him, so I couldn't refuse. They're going to bring him when they come over."

Mama was grinning the whole time she said that, so I knew she was really happy to finally have Daddy home, but I had my mouth all ready for some pizza. And now I wasn't getting any.

"Go tell Mavis to come down here; we'll have to run to Coney Island to get you two something to eat real quick because the food won't be ready for hours."

Nothing says loving like a family dinner, and ours were especially interesting for obvious reasons—blacks and Italians in the same house cooking together?

I could sell tickets.

Mavis and I were probably the only twins in the entire universe with collard greens and cannoli on the same plate (we learned long ago to grab our dessert during dinner, in case a storm blew through and we had to hightail it to our rooms to avoid the lightning).

But to get our hands on the goods, we had to endure the ritual of fussing, finger pointing, and loud accusations about whose mother country produced the best cooks.

With Daddy home, Mama didn't seem to notice. Whenever I looked her way, she was staring at him like a lovesick puppy. Even though he'd only been gone six months, it seemed like a lifetime. I missed how patient he was with us and how he always found a way to end an argument. His skills were in high demand that day because Uncle Bobby (Mama's brother) was having a showdown with Uncle Sil (Daddy's brother) over what local joint made the better pizza. This was a real sore point with Uncle Sil, who was still struggling with English since he'd only been in America a short time. His given name was Silvestro, but he said that in America things were simple, so he shortened it to Sil.

"You crazy?" yelled Uncle Sil, his fist in the air. "Augustine. He make the best pizza pie in all the world. Just like Mama in the old country."

"Well, he best go back to the old country and learn how to make it again, 'cause that mess is nasty." Uncle Bobby flipped the burgers over the stove with attitude and waved away the smoke. I expected the whole house to resemble a London fog before he was through. He had on his official grilling apron that said, "Here Comes Da Cook." After adding some hot dogs, he pointed his spatula at Uncle Sil. "Ain't nobody ever heard of a pizza with no meat on it. Augustine's pizza ain't got no meat. Who eats pizza without the meat?"

"Meat, meat. That's all you think," said Uncle Sil,

throwing up his hands. "Good pie only needs Parmesan cheese."

Uncle Bobby let out a humongous laugh. Uncle Sil waved off the conversation and headed straight to the bar. Daddy always set up a bar in the den for the family. That was one feature neither side argued about. Mama's side stocked it with gin and rum, while Daddy's brought the vodka for martinis and, of course, lots of red wine. I knew because Daddy let me help him get things ready. Mama didn't like that. She laid down the law to Mavis and me before every event: "And if I smell alcohol on your breath, I'll slap the taste buds out of your mouth."

Just for the record, I still have my taste buds.

Personally, as long as I had access to the record player and Aunt Minnie's famous sweet tea, I was fine. Most of Mama's family were southerners. They moved from Alabama in the 50s and came to Pennsylvania. Mama said the family was seeking better job opportunities, not to mention better treatment than they'd received in the South. Daddy's people immigrated to New York from Italy, and then they settled here. Mama and Daddy met in Pittsburgh while Daddy was in ROTC. Mama started college but never finished. After she and Daddy got married, taking care of us was her full-time job. Then the war came, and Daddy had to go, so Mama went to work. I thank God every night that he came home safely and in one piece.

Even though Daddy was in the service, to me, words were more powerful than weapons. I agreed with what the song said: war was good for absolutely nothing.

I dug around in Mavis's record collection to see if she had that jam. It would be perfect, and the families wouldn't disagree. I searched and searched, but I didn't find it, so I joined Mavis on the love seat.

"I saw Aunt Minnie playing with your hair." Mavis

scrunched her brows. "Face it, Camille, even our own family is hair-struck. That's like color struck only—"

"I know what it is. And just for the record, I'm not speaking to you. What you said last night about Julius was wrong, and I'm going to prove it. And as far as Aunt Minnie goes, how can her fussing over my hair be considered some sort of prejudice? She does that to me every time she comes over."

"And it doesn't even faze you, does it? Which proves my point."

I leaned close to Mavis and sniffed.

"What are you doing, trying to kiss me?"

"Just making sure you still have your taste buds."

Mavis got up, made her way to one of the makeshift tables Daddy set up for the feast, and started fixing her plate. I was still sitting in the chair considering the possibility that she might be on dope. I'd heard that some older kids were pushing pills after school. Maybe one of them talked her into trying something.

"Mavis," I said, joining her at the table, "have you ever dropped mescaline or THC, maybe?"

"Camille Marconi, have you lost your mind?"

"That's what I was about to ask you because you talk like you're high. Honestly, Mavis, this hair thing is getting funky, and not in a good way. Why can't you just support me and this contest so we can get back to normal?"

"After you tried to give me a milk bath? Nothing doin'."

She held a fork in one hand and a Chinet in the other. "Your obsession with winning this contest and trying to reel in Julius is gonna backfire on you. And for your information, I've come up with a new direction for my protest, so if things go as planned, you might not have a shampoo contest to win."

She flashed me a 'wouldn't-you-like-to-know-what-that-meant' smile and moved on to the dessert table.

"Do your tha-a-a-ng," was all I could say because her smile was right. I did want to know what she meant.

I decided to forget Mavis and go find Daddy. I looked around. There were Uncle Bobby and Uncle Sil sitting together eating and talking. Guess they got tired of arguing about pizza. Aunt Minnie and Mama were sitting on either side of their man-crazy sister, Shirl, no doubt trying to talk some sense into her before she got into another bad marriage.

Daddy's nephews—my cousins Tony and Mike—were outside, trying to get some of the neighbor kids into a game of craps. They were always looking for ways to make money.

Daddy's sister Isabella was primping, as usual, in front of the compact she never left home without, and last of all were my two grandmothers swapping Italian and Southern recipes.

The family was definitely different, but at the same time they were alike. That was the way I had always looked at everyone, as people. Not Black people, not Italian people, but people. It made me wonder what happened to Mavis and how she got so caught up in all this activism. Maybe I could've understood it if we still lived in the 60s, but things were different. In school, kids hardly talked about it. It was nothing to see Black and white kids together—in class, in the halls, and even after school at games and parties. Times had changed, and I wanted Mavis to change with them. That's why I was looking for Daddy. He'd know what to do.

I found him in the garage, getting ice from the deep freezer for the bar.

"Hey, Daddy," I said. "Can I help you take that inside?"

"Sure, my angel flower, take this bucket, and I'll get some more from the trays."

Daddy was always busy during these dinners. He never

complained about the families and seemed genuinely happy to have them around.

"So what were you and your sister up to while I was gone? Your mother says you girls haven't been too happy since that hair contest." He said.

"It's not me, Daddy, it's Mavis. She is dead set on proving *something*."

"Well, you know what I've always said. Family first, Bella."

I lowered my head, and my heart sank because I knew what that meant: Daddy expected *me* to take the first step to peace. It was just like I told Mama: no matter what kind of mess Mavis got us into, I was always the one expected to get us out of it. Like I was her big sister and not her twin. But knowing Mavis preferred protest to peace, I wondered whatever happened to my Dear Addy letter because *this* time I needed professional help.

I followed Daddy to the bar and stood by while he prepared all the glasses for a toast.

Uncle Sil turned around to see what Daddy was doing. Then he stood and made an announcement.

"Everyone, everyone listen. Raise a your glass. Fill it up. Okay, okay. Now raise a your glass to my brother whom I love, Alberto!"

"Salut, Alberto," said Daddy's side.

"Welcome home, Al," Mama said.

After the toast, Daddy and I sat in the loveseat.

"Is there something else you wanted to talk about, darling?"

"Oh, Daddy, I know what you're always saying about family and how important it is."

"Yes, it's very important."

"But what if someone in your family isn't acting like it's important?"

"You want to know what is making Mavis so determined?"

"Well, I kind of already know. That dumb audition started it all."

"Well, my love, if you really want to know what I think, it may be nothing more than your sister being pig-headed. You know where she gets that from, right?" Daddy smiled at me.

"I'm not as bad as she is, Daddy. I don't have to have my way all the time."

"Don't you?" he asked. "You are a twin, Camille, and not an ordinary twin. You are an identical twin. That is something so special. You may not want to admit it, but whatever you see in your sister is also in you." He gave me a big hug. "Now go and talk to Mavis, and be nice, okay?"

"Okay, Daddy."

Before I faced Mavis, I figured it wouldn't hurt to go back for seconds while things were calm among the family. Besides, I wasn't exactly buying all that jive Daddy was talking. He just wanted us to get along. Just like Uncle Bobby's barbecue, if I expected to ever get Mavis off my back, I'd have to light my *own* fire.

CHAPTER 8

When I woke up Saturday morning, Mavis was not in her bed. It was made. I locked my eyes on the closet doorknob: that ugly Army/Navy bag was gone. I sat up like Frankenstein come to life.

Where was she?

Mavis never got up early on Saturdays, unless we both did, and usually we'd planned it the night before, especially if something special was coming on television.

I jumped into my fuzzy, furry house shoes, grabbed my raggedy robe (which really needed replacing), and ran out the door.

At the top of the stairs, I waited. I wanted to listen for any signs of life down below. Nothing.

I took my time going down the stairs in case some surprise awaited me. Like, maybe a burglar they left behind when they ran out of the house and forgot about me.

I tiptoed into the kitchen and kept tiptoeing until I made it to the back door.

VOOM

The noise of the garage door startled me, so I stepped back and, again, waited.

Daddy burst in, "Hey there, sleepyhead." He chuckled more than spoke it, leading the way for Mama and Mavis. The third wheel had a huge smile on her face, and you *knew* what that meant: she was up to no good.

I watched as Mama and Daddy put the grocery bags on the table. Daddy never liked going grocery shopping, but he seemed genuinely happy as he handed Mama the cans of beans she stacked neatly on the pantry shelf. They both kept smiling at each other. One day me and Julius would be doing that exact same thing, in our fancy split-level home with our two kids and a dog. But enough about me. Mavis thought I wasn't looking, but I caught sight of her as she ducked back into the garage. It was time to do some investigating.

"Wait a minute, young lady," Mama stopped stacking to state her case. "Go right upstairs and get on some clothes. That garage door is wide open, and we don't need the neighbors seeing you half naked."

I looked at Daddy, and he nodded. I huffed my response and headed for the bedroom. As I climbed, I wondered, *what could I do to get Mavis to redirect her attention to a more worthy cause?* I pulled on my smiley face sweatshirt and some old Levi jeans, sure that something would come to me.

What would take her full attention?

I dug through the drawers for some sweat socks and stepped into my old pair of Keds. Ha!

It hit me. Armed with my new atom bomb, I blew down the stairs, through the kitchen, and into the garage. But what I saw made me explode.

"You just don't give up, do you?" I screamed, my eyes darting back and forth as they took in all the ammunition Mavis picked up from the hardware store. Long pieces of wood that looked like oversized popsicle sticks. Huge sheets of white construction paper and small cans of red, black, and green paint.

"Daddy! Mama!" I yelled at the top of my lungs.

"What is it, Camille?" They said in unison and rushed to the door with worry on their faces. The heat in my body rose so fast and burned so hot, all I could do was point.

Mavis had a giant stapler in one hand, a makeshift sign in the other, and deviousness all over her face.

Daddy let out a sigh, which sounded like relief. "Oh, that. She's just making some signs for your school project—"

"School project? What school project?" I crossed my arms, tapped my tennis shoe, and waited for the tale of two twins to twist off of that tongue of hers.

"You, you know which project," she said with a nervousness I've rarely seen in my suspect sister. "The one where we're gonna sell…handmade soap to…to raise money for…for the cheerleading squad." Mavis' eyes said lies, lies, lies, and I wasn't about to let her get away with this. But this time, I decided to go with my usual routine. I played along because *this* time, Camille Marconi had a plan.

"Oh," I said, as if I had forgotten. "We *did* volunteer for that project." I said this while keeping an eagle eye on Mavis, the miniature-monster-in-training. Boy, was she going to get hers.

Mavis looked at me with worry because she knew what was coming as soon as Mama and Daddy went inside.

"You two enjoy yourselves," Daddy said. Mama just waved us off, and they both returned to their stacking.

When they were safely inside, I reached for the knob to make sure the door was completely closed, then I turned and got right up in her fascist face.

"Get away from me, Camille," she said, backing up with arms outstretched, like that would be enough to keep me from beating her brains out. "If you hit me, they'll hear."

That's when I let her have it—not with a whack, but with words. "You are the lowest of the low, Mavis Marconi. You actually lied to Mama and Daddy. *Lied.* Are you on acid? What is your problem? This shampoo obsession is taking over that kinky-headed brain of yours—"

"See?" She raised her finger back. "That's what I mean, Camille. You are so full of yourself over this contest, you can't even see what's *really* going on." She continued her backward movement. "The world does not revolve around you or your hair or your wannabe boyfriend. Take off those rose-colored glasses, Camille, and get with the program—"

"What program, Mavis? Nobody at school cares about your stupid boycott. The custodian threw all those crusading cards of yours in the trash. You know why? Because nobody's gonna protest Herbal Excellence. *Nobody.*"

Daddy stuck his head out. Mama's was over his shoulder. "Come on in here, both of you."

I rolled my eyes at Mavis and left her to clean up her militancy mess. I walked right into the den and took a seat. The hot seat. The one I always took during Marconi Family Court.

Mama and Daddy took their usual seats, too. On the couch, opposite the two chairs Mavis and I normally occupy. We sat there in silence for a few minutes: them looking stern and unhappy. Me, slumped in my own attitude. We waited for Mavis, who seemed to be taking her time in the garage. "She's not gonna get rid of them." I warned, my elbow on the arm of my chair and my jaw resting in my hand. "She's gonna find a way around you."

"Hush, Camille," Mama scolded. "Don't talk about your sister like that."

I shook my head and let out a long sigh. Mama doesn't even know her own daughter. I blamed it on *Gunsmoke* and Miss Kitty.

When Mavis finally decided to join the party, Daddy stood and began with his typical speech about not tolerating intolerance and the importance of loving one another. It was a snooze fest. But I didn't act like it, that is, if I didn't want to get smacked upside the head. Especially by someone who, for the last 6 months, spent his days *blowing* other people's off.

"First, Mavis will take the stand." Daddy pulled the wooden stool into the middle of the room where testimony took place. I sank even deeper into my chair so I could prepare myself for all the crap she was gonna start spouting.

"Well, you see, Daddy, I had this idea to enter us both into the shampoo contest just to see if they would accept me *and* Camille. But they didn't accept *me*, which proved my point that they were racist pigs and—"

"Just the facts, my dear," said Daddy. "But they *did* accept your sister, is that right?"

"Yes, they did. And that's why they deserved to be boycotted because—"

"No need to go on," Daddy told her. "I understand how you feel about this. But let me ask you: did you care at all how Camille felt about it?"

Mavis glared at me.

"Mavis?" Daddy asked.

"Well, no—"

"And when she was chosen as a finalist," he continued, "were you happy for her, knowing that she had never done anything like that before?"

Now she raised her eyes to the ceiling.

"Mavis?"

"No, Daddy, I didn't, but that's because—"

"Mavis, my dear. What does Daddy always say about family?"

This was my kind of questioning. I perked up, anxious to hear her admit it.

Mavis let out a long and disgusted sigh, "Family first."

"Very good. So does that mean you do not support your sister because you are angry with someone else?"

She lowered her head and whispered, "No, sir."

"That's my little girl. Now go and take your seat. It is Camille's turn."

I jumped from my chair like I was able to leap tall buildings in a single bound. I sat on the stool and waited for my turn to tell it like it was.

"Camille," Daddy began, "how did you feel when Mavis entered the contest?"

"Well, Daddy, I was not happy because she only did it to push her personal agenda." I gawked at Mavis to let her know I was going to win this round.

"But you know your sister, and you know she is very passionate about her causes."

My brows wrinkled. *Where was this going?*

"Well, yes, Daddy. Mavis does like to throw herself into things—"

"So then, do you think you should have tried to find a compromise instead of teasing her and telling her it was a stupid idea?"

"But Daddy it *is*. I mean, whoever heard of protesting a big corp—"

"Camille." Daddy said calmly, "I didn't ask you about the corporation or the protest. I asked you if you tried to meet your sister halfway."

When I looked over at Mavis, she was grinning all silly, like she was sure to get vindicated, and I was not feeling that at all.

"No, Daddy, I didn't. Because I—"

"It doesn't matter why, but you admit you didn't?"

I poked out my lip before responding. I wanted him to see I was a hostile witness. "No, sir. I didn't."

"Alright then. Your mother and I will deliberate in the kitchen, and we will be back with our verdict."

After they left, Mavis stood and paced the room like she always did during deliberations. She couldn't stand to wait. For anything. Least of all a verdict that made sense. But judging from her testimony, I was sure that *this* time she was *not* going to come out the victor. After all, this whole thing was *her* fault.

Minutes feel like hours when you're waiting for someone, and, when translated, meant I was sweating bullets because, if the past was any indication, the longer it took Mama and Daddy to decide, the worse the punishment. Usually, it was a punishment we shared, but I was not so sure since our activities were anti-twin this time around.

When Mama and Daddy walked in, I sat up. Mavis sat down.

I followed Mama with my eyes until she took her place on the couch. I tried to read her expression. She was really good at maintaining a stone face. Since Mavis and I came to court quite often, Mama had lots of opportunity to practice. Daddy stood in the middle of the room, as usual, and read the verdict:

"After deliberating on this situation, your mother and I have agreed on what needs to be done. First, to Mavis. For not supporting your sister when she became a finalist, we are not going to require Camille to pull out..."

I looked over to see Mavis' face turn the color of cranberry sauce. I bet if I could touch her skin, my finger would sizzle.

".... We both agree it is a great opportunity for Camille, and as her sister, you should be proud and supportive."

At this point Mavis was calming down. All the way down.

"Therefore, your verdict is guilty, and you will not do anything to prevent Camille from continuing on in the Herbal Excellence contest."

Mavis crossed her arms tight, and her face looked tighter; she sat there and did not say one single word.

"Now, Camille."

I tried to look attentive and interested. There was nothing they could say to ruin *my* day since Mavis was not able to stop me from pursuing the contest OR Julius.

"You have demonstrated yourself to be against Mavis in just about every cause she has tried to support, and even though we have agreed not to force you to get involved in these causes, we do expect you to understand your sister has the right to her views."

I could live with that. So far, so good.

"Therefore, from now on, we want you to keep your opinions to yourself as they relate to those causes and show your sister some respect."

Mavis jumped from her seat. "That's it? That's all she has to do is show me some *respect*?"

"Mavisy." Mama's pet name only brought out the radical in my raving sister.

"This is so unfair. I demand a retrial. A re-verdict. A redo."

Daddy came toward her, but Mavis turned away. "I'm going to my room where I can be alone with my *respect.*"

With that, she stomped out of the den and out of my business.

Good riddance.

———

THAT NIGHT, Mavis wasted no time showing me how much she wanted my 'respect.' She laid down a duct tape line between us in our bedroom. I'd tried to tell Daddy he should have taken all that junk back to the hardware store right away, instead of waiting.

"How am I supposed to get to the bathroom?" I asked,

eyeing the line that went between our beds. "The door is on that side."

"That is *your* problem, my sister."

"This is dumb, like most of your ideas. I've got to curl my hair for tomorrow, so I'm crossing this stupid line."

As soon as I walked past her bed, an agonizing pain shot into my foot, and I let out a loud yelp.

"What the—"

"Oops," Mavis said with her hand over her mouth. "I forgot I dropped your hot rollers. Those little nubs must hurt." Then she climbed into her bed, laughing.

She had the nerve to use my curlers to get back at me. But instead of knocking her behind to kingdom come, I hobbled into the bathroom with my lips in check.

Everything I'd had to endure would all be worth it after tomorrow when I moved ahead with my one-woman conspiracy. If she thought family court was rough, Mavis would soon see that Camille Marconi was even rougher.

CHAPTER 9

n the morning, I awoke to the savory scent of Mama's famous sausage and biscuits. The way she used to cook before Daddy left. The way she *never* did while he was gone. Mavis and I subsisted on Cheerios, Frosted Flakes, or toast. And if you didn't like it, you could lump it.

After I picked up all my hair curlers, I headed downstairs because those biscuits were calling my name.

I passed the plate of sausage and eggs to Daddy, who always read the paper at the table. Sometimes he'd be so into it that he'd get food all along the bottom.

"Daddy," I said. "You're getting food on the paper again."

"Oh, am I?" He asked, like this was the first time it had ever happened.

Mavis sat next to me quietly slopping up gravy with her biscuit. She was pouting, but I didn't care. She got what she deserved, and personally, so did I.

While watching Daddy read the paper, my eye latched onto an ad that was calling for writers. Essay writers. I leaned across the table to get a closer look.

"Camille, what are you doing?" asked Mama.

"I—I was seeing how close I had to get to the paper before all the words went blurry."

Mavis made a noise that told me she didn't believe a word I'd said. But I didn't care. I needed to see what that ad was all about:

DO YOU KNOW A TALENTED TEENAGER WHO LOVES TO CRAFT? TELL US ABOUT THEM, AND THEY COULD WIN AN INTERNSHIP WITH ONE OF THESE COMPANIES

At this point I was so close to the paper I was practically standing.

"Lord, child, do you have to get that close?" Mama asked. "I'll make an appointment with the eye doctor next week."

I wasn't even listening to her because while I was reading the ad, I saw that one of the companies on the list was the crafts store that Mavis absolutely loved.

This was it. It was even *better* than my idea—which was to get her to repaint our bedroom red, black, and green. I admit it was not my taste, but at least it would have kept her busy after school and on the weekends and possibly away from any protest. But this was a thousand times better AND easier, since I was the queen of quotations, the literary laureate, the…well, you get the picture. This was my chance to get Mavis *so* busy she'd craft herself crazy and stay out of my hair *and* my contest.

I returned to my eggs with a new outlook. They tasted even better than they had just a moment ago. I'd write an essay on how talented Mavis was with all kinds of arts and crafts, and she'd be in like Flynn. I glanced at my mood ring. It was pink. That was an excellent indicator. Everything was clearer, despite the fact that next week I'd probably be wearing glasses. But being called "four-eyes" would be a small price to pay to show Mavis that the pen is mightier than the protest!

————

WHILE DADDY WAS OVERSEAS, I took over the task of getting the mail every day, so I just kept doing it when he got home. Mama didn't do it because all she got was bills. Mavis didn't do it because she never got anything. And even though I didn't either, I liked reading all the handwritten fliers selling everything from lawn care to life insurance. But on this trip down the driveway, I had a good reason to be in expectation: I opened the door, reached into the box, and pulled out a letter from Herbal Excellence. A letter addressed specifically to me. My first reaction was to hide it in case Mavis came outside, so I folded it in half and pushed it into my back pocket. And sure enough, who met me at the door with crossed arms and a critical attitude?

"So did you hear from whoever you sent that letter to, Camille? Herbal Excellence, maybe?"

I raised an eyebrow and for a split second wondered in awe over the power of twinness, because sometimes it seemed we really could read each other's minds.

"Nope. Nothing but bills for Mama and fliers for me." I said, holding the ad of a dancing slice of bread in her face. Then I strolled past her, dropped the mail on the kitchen table, and continued upstairs to the bathroom. I knew she wouldn't follow me in there.

I shut the door, pulled out the letter, and sat on the toilet to read:

Dear Miss Marconi,

Congratulations! You have been chosen as the new model for our upcoming —

I screamed before I could read the rest, which did nothing but draw attention from Mama and Mavis.

"Camille, what's going on in there? You all right?" Mama called from the kitchen. She was about to start dinner, so I knew she wouldn't come up, especially since she might see or smell something she'd rather not. But Mavis wasn't shy. I heard her platforms clicking across the wood floor, so I locked the door just as she grabbed the knob.

"I'm fine. I just stubbed my toe on the toilet."

"I bet," was her reply. "Come on out of there. I know you're up to something."

See what I mean about twinness?

Since those platforms of hers didn't move, I knew I had to. So I put the letter back in my pocket and tried to think of a good place to hide it before nightfall.

"Mavis, can you back up? I'm coming out."

I pushed the door hard.

"Ow."

"I told you to get out of the way," I said, leaving her to rub her red nose.

Then I raced to the stairs, and of course, my twin was on my heels.

"I know you got a letter, Camille, and it better not be about my protest."

I stopped before descending. "No, I didn't get a letter, and even if I did, you are on protest lockdown, remember?"

Mavis' eyes widened, which meant she understood her limits.

But Mavis was not a quitter, and judging from past experience, I knew she would find a way around it. When she went back downstairs to see what Mama was cooking, I went back to the bathroom to get the rest of my good news:

Dear Ms. Marconi,

Congratulations! You have been chosen as the new model for our

*upcoming commercial for Herbal Excellence Shampoo and
Conditioner. Our promotional staff will notify you on what day the
camera crew will arrive in New Castle. In the meantime, we would
prefer that you keep this information confidential until we come
back to town and officially announce you as the winner on May 10,
1973.*

Again, congratulations, and see you soon!
Yours,
James Stanton, Marketing Director
Herbal Excellence, a division of Curall

That last part was a letdown since I was hoping to tell the
entire school in general, and Julius in particular. Wouldn't
you know it—just when I'd gotten some leverage I could use
to get him to notice me, *apart* from being a twin. Then again,
maybe I could tell him and no one else? It could be our little
secret. I smiled just thinking about it: me, Julius, and my
newfound fame. Nothing Mavis could do would be able to
spoil *that*.

I went back downstairs with a new sense of confidence
and hoped I could keep it from showing on my face. I
wondered if not telling anyone included my parents. I
couldn't keep the secret from them. I'd wait until Daddy and
Mama were watching TV or something, then I would tell
them together. In the meantime, this bit of news would be off-
limits to Public Protester No. 1.

In the kitchen, Mavis glared at me while wielding a paring
knife she was using to peel some potatoes. That look in her
eye meant she'd love to use it on me. But I didn't show any
signs of concern. I had a secret.

"Camille, did you ever hear anything about that
audition?" Mama asked.

My eyes locked on Mavis's, but neither of us responded. *I*
didn't answer because Mavis would have a cow. *She* didn't
answer, obviously because she didn't know. So I figured I'd

better look busy. I grabbed a can opener and the three cans of tuna fish Mama set on the counter. Still not saying a word, I proceeded to crank them open.

Mama glanced at me and then at Mavis. "Well, I think it's best that you didn't win. Now maybe things will get back to normal—"

"Things will never be normal if companies like Herbal Excellence don't bend to the will of the people," Mavis blurted. "All I want is for them to feature Afros in their ads. I could care less if Camille won that stupid contest because that was *not* the point."

"Oh, it wasn't?" I shot back. "Seems to me that my losing was the MAIN thing you wanted—"

"OK, OK, that's enough," Mama said in a huff. "Remember what your father said. You need to support Camille, and Camille, you need to respect Mavis. You are sisters—"

"If I had a *real* sister, I would," Mavis said, still wielding that paring knife.

"Ditto," I said, but nothing more, because I could see in Mama's eyes she was over the whole conversation. Besides, Daddy was coming in from the den.

"You two go get washed for dinner." He said.

We both went upstairs, but in my mind, the only part of her argument that I held onto was that Mavis 'could care less' if I won. I smirked to myself, wondering whether she'd eat those words if she knew the truth.

After dinner, Mavis and I usually did our homework. Since we had two desks in our room, one on each side, we didn't disturb each other. But those desks did double duty, because when we first got them, Mavis and I made a deal:

"You don't look in my drawers, and I won't look in yours." The look on Mavis' face that day was so serious; if she had a gavel, she would have slammed it right then and there.

Case closed. And since I had a reason to stash some personal items, she couldn't reverse the verdict.

So at my desk, I slipped the Herbal Excellence letter into a drawer—the one in the middle—the one with the teeny tiny lock that could not be opened unless you had the teeny key that went with it. I kept that key on a chain around my neck, and I never, ever took it off. Not even for a bath. Mavis never told me where she hid *her* key.

Next, I pulled out my diary since it was in that same drawer, and as I was about to open it, here come da judge.

"Can I borrow your American History book?" she asked in a way that told me she was fishing. "I left mine in my locker at school."

"I can do better than that," I said with a huge smile. "I can give you the answers so you don't need the book," since said book was kept in my desk and I didn't need her snooping around trying to play like she was looking for it.

Mavis' smile turned to a frown. "Never mind. I know the answers. I just wanted to double-check them in the book."

I turned around and leaned my arm over the top of my chair. "Mavis, admit it. It is killing you to know whether I got an answer from Herbal Excellence, so I'm gonna put you out of your misery. Like I said the *first* time you asked me. No, I did not write to them, and no, I did not get a letter from them. Satisfied?"

A twinge of guilt shot through me when I turned my back, because I'd never lied to her. In fact, keeping silent about this letter was the first time. But I couldn't get over that she was not happy for me when I became a finalist, and I doubt if she'd be happy to know I actually won. When you're a twin, stuff like that is supposed to be shared, but no, Mavis couldn't handle the idea of me doing anything separate from her. Don't get me wrong, I loved my sister, but gawd, just one time I would like to be known for being something other than one half of a dynamic duo. *She just doesn't get that.*

"Maybe," she finally replied, but I knew she didn't believe me.

"Big corporations like that probably don't even get their mail," I reasoned. "I bet some little dude down in the basement opens it and only gives the big shots the real important stuff. Besides, they'd never believe a 13-year-old warning them about a protest of their products."

Mavis had no comment, which was a shock. Instead, she stuck her nose out of my business and into her homework.

I pulled out my diary and opened it to page six. That's where I kept a newspaper clipping of Julius on the George Washington Junior High School basketball team. Senior varsity, of course. He was the boy standing at the far left: tall, dark, and handsome (actually, all of them looked dark in black and white). They won the finals last year, and it was the only other picture I had of him.

It's on page six because there are 6 letters in his name — J-U-L-I-U-S. Smart, huh?

Since Mavis was still in the room and could hear anything I said, I mouthed the words to the picture, telling him that I won the contest and pretending he was happy for me. I could not wait until school tomorrow because in the morning I would be on a mission: to find him and share my good news.

CHAPTER 10

At school the next day, Mavis and I got into twin mode, just for show. Whenever we had a family disagreement, we kept it between us. That was one thing we actually *agreed* on.

It was time for the Friday afternoon ritual to begin. Students from every classroom burst forth, like fire hydrants on a hot day. The halls were as dense as Disneyland, yet everyone knew exactly where they were going. That's what bothered me the most. I *hated* where we were going. It was the worst of all junior high activities: the assembly.

It wasn't just the boring speeches or the smart kids getting awards; it was also another reminder that I was at the bottom of the heap, a 7th grader. And 7th graders had their own special place at assemblies.

"There they go," said one 8th grader as he and his classmates descended the stairwell. "Up to Peanut Heaven."

Mavis and I climbed the stairs with all the other freshmen to the dreaded balcony. I hated Peanut Heaven and all the kiddy aspects that went with it. For one, it made me feel, well, kiddy. On top of that, I had to endure the staring from down below, where the 8th and 9th graders pointed and snickered.

"Come on," I said to Mavis, leading the way to our seats. "Let's sit down front so we can see what's going on."

"You mean who's down there, as in Julius Barron."

As you probably guessed, I let that remark fall flat, just like my butt into the hard wooden seat. Then I leaned over the balcony to scan the activity below.

Bodies moved in and out of the aisles like ants. Guys and gals bumping into and walking over each other. There was something about upperclassmen: it was like they knew they were on display and were proud of it. When the bell rang, the ants scurried as they made a desperate effort to get seated before the principal walked onto the stage and signaled the end of musical chairs.

On my last scan of the floor, when my eyes finally landed on him, my heart skipped a beat. There was Julius, the divine, play-punching his teammates, all of whom were wearing basketball jackets in the school colors—blue and gold.

I wanted to wave so bad and get his attention, but with Mavis practically sitting on top of me in these skintight seats, I was doing well just to breathe on my own.

Mavis groped through her purse and pulled out a mini set of knitting needles wound round with red thread. She always used these opportunities to create something. I felt sorry for artsy people. They couldn't help it.

"What's it gonna be this time?" I whispered, figuring I may as well make conversation since I was sardined in for the next hour.

"I haven't decided," she said, head down. "Maybe I can make you a cape, Red Riding Hood, before the wolves show up to eat you."

"Cut the jive, Mavis." I grumbled. "It's getting old."

SHHHH

Someone behind us wasn't feeling it either, so I raised the peace sign without looking back. I was sure they got the message.

————

WHEN I FINALLY HEARD THE magic words—"You are dismissed"—I couldn't wait to get to the stairwell. There, I caught sight of Julius, so I stopped and held onto the railing.

"You're gonna get your face crushed, Camille. Julius is not what you think—"

"You're just jealous," I shot back.

And without saying another word, Mavis brushed by and continued down the stairs. I ignored her and put on my best smile. When Julius got close, I used my index finger to call him to me. His eyebrows went up, but he came.

"What's goin' on, Camille?" He said, flashing those Colgate-white teeth.

"I want to tell you something."

"What?" He said it with a smidgeon of impatience, so I whispered it into his ear.

"But you cannot tell anyone," I cautioned.

"Wow, Camille." That's when his mood changed. "But isn't that the company that doesn't feature Afros in their ads?"

Not him too? Talk about deflating my enthusiasm.

"Well, uh—"

"Actually, this might be cool," he said with a strange look on his face. "I gotta get to class but maybe you and I can, uh, get together after school… and talk."

Man, did I want to say 'yes,' but you *know* I had to say 'no,' and you *know* why.

"I can't after school, but maybe we can meet *before*

school…at your locker…tomorrow?" I suggested, with all ten of my toes crossed.

His eyes slid to the ceiling, like he had to think about it.

"Sure. Meet you tomorrow."

Then he did what I hadn't seen him do since I was in elementary school. He winked at me, and right away, whatever my heart was made of, it turned straight to jelly. I must have been in a purple haze, because I hung onto the railing and watched him, and his fine self, walk away, and then I felt the thud of a finger to my head.

"Stop playing," I said to Mavis, my swipe just missing that ugly Army/Navy bag.

"Come on," she called back to me. "We're gonna miss the bus."

———

ON THE RIDE HOME, I was beaming. I still couldn't believe I got Julius to meet me at his locker in the morning. That meant I had to pull out my hot rollers and Dippity-Do. My hair had to look just right for him.

"Wipe that silly smirk off your face, Camille. Julius Barron is not interested in you."

I turned my nose up at her without asking how she knew that, but of course, you *know* she told me.

"Gerald says that when they moved to Africa, Julius got really into the culture. Not like he did, I mean. But he started reading a lot about the continent, its rulers and stuff like that—"

"So?

"So, he says Julius turned into a bookworm. Started running around the house spouting philosophy and all that jive. Weird."

I leaned back and stared at her. "You're just trying to get me to stop liking him. Maybe... because *you* like him."

Mavis' eyes bugged the way girls did when you caught them in a lie. But she recovered quick and tried to lay some phony line on me about how she wasn't interested in older boys. "He's not my type anyway," she said, but it didn't compute. Something else was going on in that mind of hers, and I was intent on getting to the bottom of it.

"I see what you're doing. You think if you can convince me that Julius is a square, I'll stop liking him and maybe even pull out of the contest. Well, it won't work. Besides, he's meeting me by his locker in the morning. What does *that* tell you about his interest in books?"

Mavis shrugged and pulled out an unfinished something or other she'd been working on. It looked like a belt, but I could never be sure until she was done. "Good luck" was all she said.

We kept silent the rest of the way home. I looked over at her once or twice to see her smiling and crocheting. Little did she know that after I wrote my essay, she'd be doing a whole lot more crocheting and a lot less imposing.

———

IN THE MORNING, Mavis left me in the hall when I stopped at locker #160. She didn't say anything smart, and she didn't try to talk me out of it, which made me wonder if what she told me was true.

Why should I take the word of someone who doesn't have my best interest at heart—but who probably should?

I dismissed my doubts because soon I'd find out for myself whether Julius was a real dude or a real dud.

I stood there for another 5 minutes, worried that if he

didn't show up soon, I'd have to run to study hall. Two minutes later, someone did show up, but it wasn't Julius.

"He's not here yet?" The brother in the blue turtleneck asked me. He was as tall as a basketball player, but he wore thick black glasses, which diminished any inch of coolness he might have had to go along with that height.

"Not yet, and I've got to get going." I said, about to walk away.

"Well, if you see him, tell him we got the auditorium for our Ugandan discussion. He'll need to bring his A game if he's gonna outdebate the Idi Amin team. See ya later."

I stood there for a moment in a state of immobility. First of all, who was this dude? And second, what the heck was he talking about? As I schlepped to my first class, my disappointment in not meeting Julius was overshadowed by my concern that Mavis could be right. But rather than dwell on the negative, I decided to give Julius the benefit of the doubt. After all, maybe Basketball Brain was talking about a class project. And maybe Julius just got caught up and had a legit reason for leaving me hanging. Satisfied with my conclusion, I sat down at Mavis' table and acted as if nothing was wrong.

"So, did he show?" She asked with delight in her voice.

"S-h-h-h. No talking in study hall, remember?"

I flipped open my civics book, turned to the page on the three branches of government, and buried my head in it. I figured now was as good a time as any to learn the importance of putting a check on those in power.

While I breathed in the staleness of my textbook, I gave some thought to the possibility that my sister could be right about my Romeo. And if so, did I really want to be thrust into the spotlight of a company for which he might harbor some resentment?

Saved by the bell.

I grabbed my purse and my books and slid my chair under the table.

"If you see Julius," Mavis said with extra coolness, "tell him I said what's happenin'"

I turned my back on her remark and headed for the door. If I *did* see Julius, it would be to make plans for our future. No boy who looked like he did could possibly resist a superstar like I was about to be. No boy on earth, and *especially* not in New Castle.

CHAPTER 11

I f I intended to do this essay thing right—and I did—I had to do a little investigative snooping. Which, when translated, meant I needed some evidence of Mavis' exploits to send along with my letter. So I slipped my Kodak Instamatic into my pocket and waited for the right opportunity. After all, a picture was worth one thousand words, and I had no plans to write an epic. Seeing was believing. Once they got a load of how talented Mavis was, she'd be a shoo-in for that internship, and I could finally boot her out of my love life.

Saturday afternoons were pretty standard for us: after we'd watched cartoons and eaten our morning cereal, I always went to my room to read or write in my diary. Mavis, on the other hand, made a beeline to the basement, where most of her crafts were kept. Just imagine somebody like Picasso or Rembrandt—paint and brushes strewn all over the place, piles of oversized canvas, and discarded false starts. Except for our weekly ritual of clothes washing, Mavis pretty much bogarted the basement. Mama and Daddy agreed she could have it all to herself since it was not within eyesight of anyone who happened to pay us a visit.

So, as usual, it was in the darkness of her dungeon where I found Mavis that Saturday, but this time I wasn't down there for dirty clothes. I was waiting for my sister to get into the groove and create something I could feature on film.

"What do you want, Camille?" She asked, eyeing me over the top of a huge crazy quilt she had hanging on a clothesline. It was filled with colorful patches of flowers, peace signs, and the long-legged dude from the Keep On Truckin' T-shirts.

"I came to…get a load of clothes…for Mama." I said, making my way to the washing machine while retrieving my Kodak. Once I got far enough away, but close enough for a good shot,

CLICK

She looked up, and I put my hands behind me.

"What was that?" She said, darting her head around the quilt.

"What was what?" I opened the washing machine and stuck my head in. "I didn't hear anything," I echoed. When I pulled my head out, she was behind that quilt again. "I'm just gonna book and let you do your thing."

I ran up the stairs and shut the door behind me. This was going to be harder than I thought. One picture wouldn't be enough to show those essay folks how creative Mavis was, so I decided to get creative myself.

Up in our room, there was more evidence of my sister's endeavors, so me and my camera went wild. Thank goodness I had a few Magicube flashes left. These pictures had to be impressive.

The paint-by-number mountain scene on our wall.
CLICK
The pink and yellow bunny rabbit hook rug
CLICK
The closet is full of tie-dye T-shirts.
CLICK

And the icing on the cake: Mavis' crochet version of the Pointer Sisters' 40s-style earrings.

CLICK

Now I had everything I needed, so I sat down to write:

Dear Essay Sponsor,

My name is Camille Marconi, and I am writing about my fantastic twin sister, Mavis. She is a whiz at crochet, macrame, hooked rugs, quilting, and paint-by-number, but her specialty is tie-dye T-shirts. Mavis would be perfect for this internship because she is totally committed to being committed. When Mavis puts her mind to something creative, no one can top her or stop her. She is simply incredible. If you do not choose her for this internship, you will be making a grave mistake and losing out on a once-in-a-lifetime talent!

P.S. I have enclosed some photos of her most recent work so that you can see for yourself. Please pick Mavis Marconi.

Sincerely,

Camille Marconi, Proud Twin Sister

After reading it over three times for spelling errors, I stuffed it into my suede purse. I had to get the pictures developed first and that's where Mama would come in.

Sooner or later she'd have to go to the store, and I could volunteer to go with her. That time came the very same day.

"I think we're out of toilet paper again." I hinted at the kitchen table while Mama prepared dinner.

"Really? I just bought some last week, didn't I?"

I shrugged. "There isn't any more in the bathroom," I said sheepishly, knowing I hid all the rolls in the clothes hamper.

So just as I suspected, Mama headed to the bathroom to check, with me following close behind.

"Huh?" She said, scratching her head. "You girls use too much; that's all there is to it."

She gave me a disapproving look. "I'll just have to go get some then."

"Can I go too?" I asked. "I can help you remember any other stuff you mighta forgot."

While Mama grabbed her coat and hat, I grabbed my suede purse with the letter and the 110 film I took out of my camera. Once we got to the A&P, I went in with her but headed straight to the area where they developed film.

"Can I get this back by Friday?" I asked the man behind the counter.

"Sure. It should be ready by then." He placed my cartridge in a paper bag and dropped it down a chute. I'd use my allowance to pay for it.

"Where have you been, Camille?" Mama asked when I met her in the checkout line.

"I was in the magazine section...looking at *Seventeen*. You know I always go there, Mama." I said, putting her items on the conveyor belt. I noticed she'd gotten four rolls of toilet paper, and I wondered if they'd fit in the bathroom cabinet that was already overflowing with towels, washcloths, and the six rolls I'd hidden in the hamper.

Outside, I helped Mama put the bags in the car. "I'll take the cart back." I put one foot on the back of the metal cage, pushed with the other, and rode my way to the store entrance. I left the cart at the door, and Mama pulled around to pick me up.

Mission accomplished.

Now all I had to do was wait for that film to develop, drop the letter in the mailbox, and bingo! After that, all I needed was for somebody to read my jubilant piece of journalism and give my sister the internship of her dreams.

CHAPTER 12

That night, while Mavis and I listened to the radio, I imagined how wonderful it would be to step out on that Herbal Excellence stage as they announced to the world that Camille Marconi was the new Herbal Excellence shampoo model. I could see myself dressed in a fly ball gown with crinoline all around and sequins on the top. Like Cinderella. I might even wear a tiara. I'd walk out to my waiting fans, waving my gloved hand to all the adoring TV viewers. Then I'd swing my mighty mane and make Julius go insane. Stephanie and Cynthia were already making plans for me to see a beautiful dress at Troutman's they said would be perfect if Mama and Daddy would buy it. The whole thing made me chuckle.

"What are you laughing at Camille?" Mavis said it like she was more annoyed than interested. "There's nothing funny about The Four Tops."

"I wasn't laughing at the song. I was just…laughing, that's all." Then I rolled over to face my twin. "Haven't you ever heard the saying, 'laughter is the best medicine'?"

She glared at me and said, "People who laugh for no

reason are usually wearing a straitjacket, and brain surgery is their medicine."

I rolled back and decided to just enjoy the music and my moment. A moment not even an evil twin could destroy.

———

IT TOOK Mavis two days to get her act together with me, but I knew she had to snap out of it sooner or later. Not just because twins cannot stay mad at each other, but also because it was time to restock our supply of hair products, and Mavis never had any bread.

We walked down to Hite's Dairy since it was right down the street. Hite's carried all kinds of things: milk, potato chips and dip, ice cream, deodorant, and magazines. Everything. Sometimes Mama would send us down there to get stockings. Hite's also had one aisle full of hair products—for Afros, too. We took our time shopping, strolling up one aisle and down the other looking for Aqua Net and Afro Sheen. That's when I spied one of my favorite products.

"Look, they got in more Clairol Condition. I love this stuff," I said, picking up the box to admire the new jar of deep conditioner. I was so busy talking to the box that I didn't notice Mavis staring at another product.

Oh no.

Mavis had gotten her hands on the new Herbal Excellence shampoo bottle. She was clutching it so tight I thought she'd blow the top off, so I snatched it out of her hand.

"Mavis, I know you're upset, but let's face it. It is what it is."

"What this is can only be described as an abomination."

Oh brother, here comes the drama.

My stomach started tying itself into knots. Why did we have to come here and see that straight-haired girl sitting on a bench with that cute white boy? I immediately pictured myself there with Billy Dee Williams, in that tulip garden they always show on TV, thinking she was obviously last year's model. She was cute, though, but the effect it was having on Mavis was not.

"Come on," I said. "Let's get our stuff and go."

I literally dragged Mavis to the counter, paid for our products, and pulled her through the door.

She stormed on ahead of me, as she usually did when things didn't go her way.

"Wait up, Mavis," I said. "This is getting out of hand."

Mavis whipped around to face me so abruptly that I almost slammed into her. Then she took a deep breath, turned her back to me, and kept walking. That was strange. I expected to get yelled at for something that was not my fault. But not this time. In fact, she didn't breathe another word all the way home. I threw up a quick prayer asking God to get my film developed early so I could mail my essay. If I didn't get Mavis' mind to move onto other matters, there was no telling what would happen.

"The A&P called, Camille," Mama said once we got back. "You got some film to pick up."

Mavis didn't even hear her. She stomped up the stairs and slammed our bedroom door.

"Can you take me to go get it, Mama? It's kind of important."

On the way back, we stopped at the post office so I could finally get the essay mailed. In the car, Mama gave me the third degree:

"What's this all about, Camille? Does this have something to do with that contest?"

Perfect. Glad she thought of it.

"Yes, actually. It does. They asked for a few more photos so they could make a final decision."

"Well, that's wonderful, dear. I know you are very excited. But what about Mavis? I hope you two are done fighting over this thing."

"Oh, we're fine," I lied. "She's just mad because Hite's didn't have her favorite oil sheen in stock."

Mama just shook her head and drove home. I sat back and tried to count how many lies I'd told this week and to how many people. Not to mention the truths I had yet to tell. I knew Mama and Daddy would find out that I won sooner or later, and the last thing I wanted was for them to find out from someone other than me. But more importantly, what would Mavis do when she found out? The only person who knew my secret was Julius, and I knew he wouldn't tell. In fact, I'd remind him again at school tomorrow as soon as I got him to tell me why he'd stood me up.

CHAPTER 13

About a week later, Julius and I agreed to meet in the girl's gym. There was no class in there at the time. Before school, I'd slipped a note through the slot in his locker door, so he'd know where to go. I didn't tell the Jewels because, well, they'd be trying to sneak a peek at us, and I didn't want anything to go wrong. They were my girls, but he was about to be my man.

"I'm really sorry about the other day," he said with sincerity in his voice. "I had to go to talk to my history teacher."

"It's OK, Julius; I knew you'd have a good reason." I said, acting all shy and 7th-graderish. I hated that I didn't know the ways of the 9th grade girls, or my answer might've gotten me a kiss or something. As it was, he just grinned at me like I was his baby sister.

"Anyway, now that we're together—"

"Together?" I said with wide eyes.

"No, I mean here. We can discuss a few things."

"Oh, OK." I said with not-so-wide eyes.

He looked at me but not in a romantic way. It seemed like

he was studying me or something. Then he said, "Have you ever heard of apartheid?"

"Whose hide?"

He laughed one of those 'I'm-not-surprised-that-you-didn't-get-it' laughs. "No, not that kind of hide. Apartheid. It's a form of slavery Black people in South Africa are facing."

That whole comment made the ends of my brows smash together. Not because I didn't understand it. I did. But because he said it. Julius Barron. My dream date. Was sitting there with me, in that huge empty room, with no one else around, and asking me about African oppression? I thought *Gerald's* rap was weak. I had to blink twice to snap myself out of it because I must've been mistaken.

"Uh...maybe" was all I could say.

Then he took my hand. My *hand* said, "Good, because I think that you could play the perfect part in my—"

RING

"Shoot. Gotta go," he said, then he stood, jumped off the bleachers, and ran out of the gym.

NOOOOOOOOOOO!

"Julius," I called after him, but it was too late. "Come back and tell me what perfect part I can play in your life." No one heard me but me.

"Darn it." I gathered my books, my suede purse, and my heart off the top bleacher and headed to class.

I will never forgive whoever invented the school bell.

I couldn't quite put my finger on it, but something was not right about Julius. What did apartheid and our being perfect for each other have in common? I didn't have a clue. Then I figured maybe it was his way of easing into asking me to give him a chance. But apartheid? I decided that as soon as school let out, I would go to the library so I could look it up.

———

"Why are you going to the public library?" Was my twin's first question. She knew that any research I ever had to do, I made a point to get done *during* school, not *after*.

And you *know* I couldn't tell her the truth. Jiminy Christmas. The lies and secrets were piling up, and to be honest, I was not feeling it. But of course, I *had* to do it. Being honest would just make matters worse.

Where in the heck was the response to my essay?

I walked ahead of Mavis, who insisted on coming.

"I need to do some research myself," she said to my back, her voice trying to catch up to my ears. But I was rushing to get there since it was still a little chilly out and I really didn't want to talk. Only one more block, so I wrapped my knit scarf tight and kept my lips tighter (they were dry, and since I didn't have any Vaseline, I had to hold them inside my mouth to keep them from cracking).

The New Castle Public Library was old, and I mean *o-l-d*. The building had been there since 1938; the outside was a dusty green like old statues that used to be copper. Mama said the building was a post office before it became the library. I don't know why they just didn't build a new one.

Inside, the stairs click-clacked like marble, and the banister swirled upward like it could reach the sky. Searching for information on apartheid was going to be tricky because I never used those big wooden drawers with the cards in them, but I knew that my answers were in there somewhere.

I went straight to the front desk to get help, and Mavis was on me like white on rice.

"I thought you had some research to do." I asked, gawking at the minute amount of distance between her face and mine. "Why don't we meet upstairs when we're both done?"

"Hmph," was her reply before she left me alone with the librarian.

"Can I help you with something?" The nice lady said. She wore a black and green wool jacket and matching skirt, and her hair was short and wavy. No glasses.

Aren't librarians supposed to wear glasses?

"I'm trying to find out all I can about apartheid. It wouldn't have anything to do with romance, would it?" I smiled longingly as her expression changed from pleasant to surprised.

"Not the last time I checked," she said. Then she went to that big wooden dresser with all the cards. She came back with a few.

"You can find all the information on apartheid in the social studies section, down the hall and to the left. Aisle 9."

I took my time getting there because my eyes were searching for Mavis. I didn't want her sneaking up on me in such a serious section as Aisle 9.

The thin walkway between the tall cases smelled ancient, and the books were more of the same. I ran my finger along each title until I found what I was looking for.

Most of the books barely mentioned apartheid and were mainly about history, and as I opened each one to read, I got bored really quick. Then I saw a novel. The spine said, *Cry, the Beloved Country* by Alan Paton. Other than that, nothing. I decided to check out the novel since, for one, it didn't look boring, and two, it might have some romance in it to help me understand Julius a bit more.

At the checkout desk, Mavis had a stack of books:

How to Crochet a Purse in No Time Flat

The Hippie's Guide to Tie-Dying Anything

Paint Your Way to Paradise

For the Love of Yarn

"That doesn't look like research to me," I said, trying to find another librarian to check out my lone text.

"That's how much *you* know. Mama said I got a call today.

I am the new intern at World of Crafts. So there." She stuck out her tongue, then realized the librarian was watching. "Sorry."

"What? I mean, when? I mean, you just said when—"

Mavis raised a suspicious eyebrow. "What do you care? But if you must know, there was some contest at the craft store, and apparently, I won. See, you aren't the only one who can win things, Camille."

"That's...fantastic," I said, hoping I didn't sound phony. I put the novel in my purse and locked my arm in hers as we walked out the door. "I am so happy for you."

She pulled from my grasp. "What's the deal, Camille? Why all of a sudden are you happy for me?"

I got right up in her face and said, "Because, if I am happy for *you*, then maybe, just *maybe*, you could be happy for *me*?"

I picked up the pace and got ahead of her so she could let those words marinate in that monotonous mind of hers. As I walked, I thought about how fast those essay folks got that whole thing done. Whoever ran that joint needed to run the entire country.

Step aside, Nixon; the crafters are comin' acha.

At home, I threw off my jacket and scarf and took my suede purse to our room. I could not wait to dig into that apartheid novel to see if it would give me any insight into what Julius was *about* to tell me. But Mama and Daddy had other ideas.

"Come in here, Camille," Daddy said from the den. "Mavis has some big news to share with the family."

I scratched the back of my neck and smirked. For my sister's sake (not to mention my culpability), I had to act like I didn't know the 'good news,' and then I had to act surprised and happy to hear it.

We all sat down in the den, as we usually did when someone was about to share good news with the family. I remember when we were 6 and lost our first front tooth; we shared that in the den. Or the time Daddy got his new Elektra 225. That was really good news.

"OK, Mavis, go ahead and tell us." Daddy said, beaming from his seat on the sunken couch. Mama sat next to him, and they held hands. They looked so cute.

"Well, I really don't know how it happened—"

I coughed, but I didn't mean to; it just came out. Mavis gave me that 'do-not-interrupt-me-again' look.

"Tell Camille about the phone call, Mavis." Mama urged.

"Yeah, that's the weirdest part. I do remember filling out a form or something the last time I went into World of Crafts, but I thought it was to win some free yarn—"

"Get to the good part." Mama was anxious, which I thought was hilarious. If only she knew.

"OK, OK. Well, anyway, I got a call. I mean, Mama did, and they said I won an internship for the rest of the school year. That means—"

"It means Mavis is going to learn the business of running a business," Mama chimed in. "Isn't that wonderful, Camille?"

"Solid," I said, grinning from ear to ear at her good news. "So, Mavis, how much time is this internship going to take exactly?" I put my chin in my hands and waited for *my* good news.

She paused and stared at me for almost a whole 10 seconds, then she seemed to blow off whatever it was she was thinking. "I'll be going into the store on Saturdays—when my homework is done—and on Sundays. Pretty much all afternoon." She squinted and gave me that stare again. "I might even go after school if Mama and Daddy can take me for a few hours."

"Of course we can, dear," Mama said, beaming.

"We will work it out somehow," said Daddy.

"Wow, that's great." I said, still smiling. "This is going to be the best—I mean, for you and your crafting career."

"Yes," said Daddy. "We are so proud of you, Mavis."

Then Mama and Daddy roped us all into a family hug, but Mavis kept her eye on me, and I knew something was working on her mind.

That night, I lay in bed and read. And read. And cried. And read. And read some more.

"What's this got to do with me and Julius?" I wondered aloud—and quietly, because by now Mavis had fallen asleep. She never even tried to find out what I was doing. Strange. Well, maybe not. To be honest, I'd kept the covers over my head as I read, because I was not in the mood for a political discussion. I was on a romance mission. One that, unfortunately, failed.

She hadn't said a word about protest or Herbal Excellence or anything since we went to Hite's the other day. I was sure it was the new internship. That, when translated, meant my plan was working.

This book, though, had zero romance and 100% sadness. I was confused because this story of a pastor and his son was horrible. I mean, it was well told, but it was way too sad and not a smidgeon of romance in the entire thing. Well, actually there was Absalom and his girlfriend, but their love affair didn't last due to his crime. In fact, all the book talked about was how their oppression under the Dutch government led each of them to desperation and loss. I lay up in bed and thought about the book all night. Racking my brain to make the connection between apartheid, Julius, and me. Until finally I realized there was no connection. Whatever he had to say to me must've been something entirely different. Something that had nothing to do with romance. Or maybe... it had nothing to do with us?

CHAPTER 14

My elation over Mavis' new distraction might have been coming across a little too strong. Mavis seemed more distrusting of me lately than she had the day I hugged the mailbox when I wrote to Dear Addy. (That's a correspondence that probably ended up in the dead letter office). Mrs. Van Austen probably doesn't even read those letters. The ones in the paper were likely from folks who worked for her and did it to keep people reading. I wouldn't be surprised if they were all made-up stories by would-be writers trying to get some attention. After all, some of those letters sounded really pathetic.

But at least Mavis' plans to protest Herbal Excellence were finally a distant memory, what with all the creating she had to do for her internship. When Mavis wasn't *at* the store, she was making products *for* the store. Our basement was humming night after night as she churned out one doodad and then another. My head was spinning, and I knew her hands must've been aching. But crafting was her passion, so Mavis persevered, and she never complained. That is, until one day when she got a call from the essay sponsors.

"Yes sir, I am enjoying my internship at World of Craft."

She said to whoever was on the other end of the line. "I am learning so much."

My timing was off because I came into the kitchen for a snack at the exact time that whoever she was talking to asked her about the essay. The essay—she knew nothing about. The essay she discovered *I* had written.

"Oh," she said, her eyes thinning. "That's my *sister...*" Mavis grimaced at me when she emphasized the word 'sister.' "...always saying great things about me." Mavis' nostrils expanded and her lips pursed, which was my cue to skip the jelly and be happy with half a peanut butter sandwich. I flew out of the kitchen, up the stairs, and then locked myself in the bathroom.

I chewed slowly and carefully while I sat on the toilet so I could hear what was going on outside the door.

Mavis was downstairs, screaming something. Mama's voice and then Daddy's. I had to stop chewing altogether to hear any more.

BANG went Mavis' fist against the door, which startled me. I jumped off the toilet seat and dropped what was left of my sandwich. *Shoot.* I stared at it, but I knew I couldn't eat it.

"Camille, get out here right now. Get out here, 'cause I'm gonna kill you."

"Mavisy," Mama's voice was calm, but that was only because Daddy was home.

"Camille," said Daddy, "we are all going downstairs, so come out of there and join us, capisci?"

Daddy's voice was angry, and that scared me. He never says 'capisci' unless one of us has screwed up—and guess which one *that* was?

My hand trembled as I reached for the half-eaten sandwich lying on the floor. I dropped it into the toilet and flushed. A part of me was afraid to unlock the door. For all I

knew, Mavis was standing out there, maybe wielding some
blunt instrument.

I leaned my ear into the door, and when I felt the coast
was clear, I came out. I cautiously peeked into our bedroom.
No one was there. When I got to the hall, no one was there
either.

"We are waiting, Camille," Daddy called from the den.

I took each step as if it were my last, holding tight to the
banister and praying that my behind wasn't going to be on
fire in a few.

I peered into the den at three serious faces.

"Come, sit down, Camille," said Daddy, motioning for me
to take a seat in the chair next to Mavis. I hesitated. "Sit
down." He said, and I did.

"What happened?" He asked. "I hear you entered Mavis
into a contest without asking her? What is going on with you
two and contests?"

"I didn't enter her into anything," I defended. "All I did
was write those people an essay telling them how talented
my sister was and that I thought she'd make a great intern—"

"You just wanted to keep me from protesting that contest
of yours—"

Daddy stood, "That's enough, Mavis. You know the rules;
you'll have your turn."

"So that's the only reason?" Daddy raised a brow at me.

"Well, no."

"See? She admits it—"

"Mavis, if I have to talk to you once more." That shut her
up. "Go on, Camille."

"OK. OK. I *did* want her to get this internship, so she'd
stop raggin' on my contest—"

"Your contest?"

"I won," I blurted. "Yes. I won." I turned to Mavis. "Did
you hear *that*? I *won*. I got the letter last week, but they told

me not to tell anyone until they come back to town to announce it."

Mama's hands covered her mouth. "Oh, my baby."

Daddy came right over and gave me a hug.

As for Mavis, I could see the smoke coming out of her ears.

"Mavis," Daddy said, "Stop sitting there pouting and congratulate your sister." He walked to the chair and stood over her. "You like that internship, I know, because you've been working hard these past few weeks. So regardless of how you got it, it's been good for you, right?"

Mavis' expression was smug, which meant she agreed, but she wasn't going to admit it.

"So be glad for your sister's success and be happy that you are doing something you love." He returned to the middle of the room. "Now let's all go to Augustine's for some pizza."

"Can we go to the Ember Club instead, Daddy?" I asked because, as far as I was concerned, this was a special occasion, and everybody knows that the lamb on the rod at the Ember Club is special.

"OK," he said. "Lamb it is."

The ride to the south side took a minute, but the food at the Ember Club was worth it. Daddy knew Harry, the owner, who always greeted him with free drinks and free fries for Mavis and me. As soon as we hit the parking lot, the charred smell of lamb roasting over an outdoor grill took my breath away. I was glad that the weather was warming up since it allowed me to linger a while with that smell. Mavis and I never disagreed over lamb on the rod. Next to Augustine's pizza, it was our favorite food, but it was not something we got every day, because eating at the Ember Club was not cheap. Like I said, today was special.

Daddy loved the peppers and garlic. Mama loved the

fragrant oil. Mavis and I loved the Syrian bread. I liked to dip mine into the oil. It was yummy.

It was the first time in a long time that we all had the chance to eat out and enjoy each other. Though Mavis was still not totally feeling me, it was cool because the food kept us all busy. Yet I could not help but wonder what her next move would be, knowing that I won the contest *and* that our parents would not approve of her protesting it. I glanced up from my lamb to look into her eyes. She didn't say a single word. And you *know* what happens when Mavis gets quiet…

———

AT HOME THAT NIGHT, I was feeling pretty confident that maybe Mavis and I might be able to bury the hatchet and move on with our twinly lives, but as we were sitting on our beds listening to our favorite radio program, she seemed to be really focused on the box. Staring at it as if the DJ was going to jump out and broadcast from our bedroom.

Then she said something that sealed it for me: "I wonder how to contact a radio station."

After that, she pulled back her covers, climbed under them, and dropped her head on the pillow. And since the lights were already out, I couldn't see her expression—and thank goodness she couldn't see mine—because after that statement, I knew confusion and fear was all over it.

CHAPTER 15

Mavis and I were sitting in the lunchroom when I peeped Julius in the doorway. He was coming toward us, and that gave me the willies. I wondered what he was going to say. He never finished what he started in the gymnasium, and he definitely needed to explain why it was so important for me to know what apartheid was. When he got close to the table, my mouth opened to speak, but Mavis beat me to it.

"Hey J, I hear you're talking about the Black People's Convention on the debate team next week." She said, ignoring me as if I didn't exist. "I can dig that."

"Right on," he said, while keeping his eyes on me. "I was just coming over to talk to Camille about it."

"Me?" I said, at the same time that Mavis said, "Her?"

"Yeah," he slung his leg over the lunch table bench and sat across from me. "I wanted Camille to come and help me in the debate, since I think she would appreciate the importance of our need to check the white establishment in South Africa," he said to Mavis. Then he directed this revelation at me. "Sort of like what you're doing by being in that Herbal

Excellence contest, Camille. I can dig your strategy to bring them down from within—"

"What?" This time Mavis and I both said it.

"I was really proud when you told me you won—" he said.

Mavis glared at me. "You told him you won?"

"Oh, did I blow it, Camille? He said, eyes wide open. "Was I not supposed to tell?"

"She knows already," I said. "Everybody does." I felt myself deflating.

"Well, anyway, I hope to see you at the debate, Camille. That's what I wanted to ask you in the gym the other day. If you'd come. Maybe afterward, we can discuss your plans for the big shake-up."

Again, I opened my mouth, but he was gone before anything could come out.

Mavis stood. "Did I hear that right? Did he say that you—Camille Marconi—who loves the straight and silky—plan to take down a corporation over a hairstyle?"

I waved her off. "I never said that. He just assumed it, I guess. Since we're *twins*."

That's when Stephanie and Cynthia came rushing over to our table.

"Is that true, Camille?" Stephanie asked. "Are you using *our* contest to prove some militant point for...*her*?"

Mavis didn't say a word. Just turned to me with a simple grin and raised brows, like she wanted to know the answer, too.

Cynthia stood over me with her hands on her hips.

My eyebrows rammed into each other. "What? No. Of course not."

Stephanie sighed. "Whew, girl. I was about to say. I should've known that dumb jock got it backwards. You are the last person on earth to give a hoot about stuff like that."

Cynthia gave Stephanie a wink. "Clothes and makeup are all you care about, right, Camille? Which means they are *way* more important than power signs and protests." Cynthia rested a hand on my shoulder. "Camille may be shallow, but she's one of *us,* and we love her *and* her empty head." They laughed and went back to their table.

Mavis and I didn't say another word for the rest of our lunch. Both of us were slowly chomping on ham and cheese, but my mind was racing.

Is that really who I am? I mean, it's true that at 13, I don't really think about anything more serious than which kicks to wear with which outfit or which new hair product to try next. But they called me shallow. If I'm shallow, what do they think they are?

"What's wrong?" Mavis asked, shaking me out of my thoughts. "Girlfriends got your number, don't they?" She lowered her sandwich when I didn't respond. "Come on, Camille, I know you're not empty-headed, like them. But after all, they ARE your friends, and remember what Mama always says about the company you keep." Then she smirked and resumed munching.

———

I wasn't feeling any better when we got home from school, but Mavis didn't try to rub it in. So as usual, I checked the mailbox and to my surprise, there sat a letter addressed to Camille Marconi, and it came from Addy Van Austen. I tore it open right there.

Dear Taunted Twin,

After reading your letter, I had to do some soul searching myself. I don't know if you were aware, but I am a twin, too. My sister and I have not spoken in years, and I must admit the issue was similar to the one you are facing with your twin. I understand that you are concerned that your sister is doing something that could cause trouble for the shampoo company. Truthfully, there is not much she can do to force them to feature a certain hairstyle, so I would not be too concerned about that. As for your relationship with her, that can be addressed. The best thing you can do is try to support her instead of criticizing her. Try to see things from her point of view. Maybe then you will be in a better position to help her see your side of things. The goal is for the two of you to come to some kind of common ground, because that is the first step to solving this rift between you. Always remember that blood is thicker than water, and with all the external forces attacking families today, you must work harder than ever to maintain your ties.

Thank you for your letter.

Sincerely,

Addie Van Austen

This was *not* the letter I wanted to read after ripping it from its envelope in anticipation. No matter whose advice I'd sought, it always ended up the same. Get along with her. Didn't they know I'd tried that? And when Daddy told her to let me alone, did she? No. She may not be acting on her plans right now, but I've known Mavis since we were born, and she was not through yet.

I took the letter inside and sat the rest of the mail on the table. Mama and Daddy could see I was sulking; I guess that's why they asked me what was wrong. I handed Daddy the letter. I didn't even bother to explain. He read it, and then I saw him look at Mama.

"Why don't the three of us take a little walk?" Daddy said. Mama nodded. I grabbed my jacket. Mavis was already in the basement working on something for her internship, so we didn't bother to tell her we were leaving.

The sun was in its descent but still shining. The air was crisp but not cold. 'Sweater weather,' Mama called it.

"The perfect evening for a little stroll," Daddy said. "I

missed taking these walks with you," he told Mama. "Nice and peaceful."

They walked close beside me, holding hands. I shoved mine in my jeans, knowing that this tranquility was just the precursor for something much more disturbing: a talk about me and my sister.

I lallygagged along, kicking stray stones or crunching leaves under my feet. After a while, I'd almost forgotten why we were walking, and then Daddy put his arm in mine.

"Did I ever tell you how me and your mother met?" I gazed up at him and nodded.

"Yes, Daddy. You met in Pittsburgh when you were in ROTC."

Daddy and Mama looked at each other, then Mama said, "That was the story we told you when you were little."

My brows frowned. "So how did you meet?"

"Before I went to the Army," said Daddy, "I used to work at a little Italian place on the Southside, and your mother would come in sometimes with her friends."

I smiled at Mama because she was blushing.

"I don't think she realized it, but I used to catch her staring at me between her bites of pizza."

"I did not," Mama scolded.

"Yes, you did, and that was fine, because I would stare at her too when I wasn't busting tables or washing the dishes." He said, smiling at her. "So, I got up the nerve to ask her to go skating with me at the local roller rink—"

"Your father was a horrible skater. He could hardly stand up."

"That's because all those boys who liked you would ram me into the wall with their fancy footwork."

Mama giggled. "Man, those boys could dance on those skates. You should've seen them, Camille."

"Yes, you should have," Daddy smirked but continued

with his story. "So anyway, that evening, I took your mother to another restaurant. After not doing so well skating, I had to impress her. So, we went to one on North Hill. When we got there, the waiter looked at us, but he did not show us to a table. So, I said to your mother, I said, 'What is going on? Does he not see us standing here?'—"

"And I told your father he was not going to seat us because I was Black."

"Well," said Daddy, "I was not going to take that lying down, so I grabbed your mother's hand, and I found a table myself."

"Wow," I said. "What happened next?"

"The waiter came over and told us that we could not sit at that table and tried to send us to a table in the back, very close to nobody." As Daddy talked, Mama lowered her head. "But I refused, and asked for the manager—"

"And what happened when the manager came?" I asked, enthralled in this new story.

"He came, and he told us to leave. And you know what else he said?" Daddy placed his hand on Mama's arm.

"It's OK, dear," she said to him.

Daddy continued, "He called her a nigger and me a nigger lover and threatened to call the police if we did not get out of his restaurant."

My eyes bugged. Not just because of what happened to my parents, but because I had never heard Daddy use that word. *Ever.*

"What did you do, Daddy? Did you beat him up?"

"No. I told him he was a fatheaded pig—"

"And a few Italian words I didn't understand at the time," Mama said.

"I won't repeat them either," Daddy said. "But the point is, we left, and we were happy to go, because we did not want to give our business to a restaurant—or even a *company*

—that did not consider us to be as worthy of their service as anyone else."

Daddy stopped walking, and his eyes met mine. "Do you understand the story, Camille?"

I stood there. Eyes closed, feeling the cool breeze on my face, blowing my hair, and I said, "Yes, Daddy. I think I understand now."

Then they both hugged me. The three of us locked arms and headed home.

———

I DIDN'T GO in the house right away. I sat on the porch steps. I just wanted to be alone. It burned me up what happened to Mama and Daddy. Especially Mama. I bet she wanted to slug the guy, too. I'd heard other stories like that about the 50s, especially down south. But I never thought anything like that could happen to my family. Or to anyone up north. It was just like I told Mavis: Black kids and white kids did things together at school, and none of the Jewels ever said anything negative about Black people. But I agreed with Daddy about that restaurant. I'd never go back there either.

I sat with my face in my hands, thinking. About the contest. About what Stephanie and Cynthia said about me, and about not letting people get away with being prejudiced. To be honest, I never thought of Herbal Excellence that way. To me it was just shampoo. But I guess maybe it wasn't just shampoo. Maybe it was more. Maybe it's just not cool to let them think it's OK. And if they *did* think it was OK, and no one said it wasn't, maybe they'd do even *more* things that didn't include Black people or any other people.

As soon as I got home, I knocked on the basement door, but Mavis didn't answer. So I figured she was in our room. When I got there, she was on the phone, and when she saw me, she put the receiver in its cradle—just hung up—like she didn't want me to know who it was.

"Where'd you guys go?" She asked in a nervous voice.

"Walking. Who were you talking to?" I asked, my brow raised.

She moved away from the phone and clumsily picked up a book that was lying on the nightstand. "No one. It was...the wrong number." She said, thumbing through the pages.

Normally, I would have given her the third degree for that bald-faced lie, but after Daddy's story, I just let it slide. I wanted to do what Dear Addy said: to understand my twin. No matter how much time and effort that might take.

But since she wasn't going to be forthcoming about the phone, I grabbed the latest Spiegel's catalog and fell onto my bed. I used the quiet time to find a nice outfit for the contest announcement. The Jewels were let down when I told them what Mama said—that the dress at Troutman's was too expensive. Regardless, May 10 was just a month away, and I still wanted to look as fine as wine on that stage.

"What are you doin'?" She finally asked. "I thought you spent your allowance?"

"I did," I said. "Mama and Daddy are going to get me something to wear for the big day—"

"For what big day? The day you embarrass the whole family by accepting the role of Miss Ann for Herbal Excellence?"

You'd have been proud to see how I reacted to *that* line. I could have gone off on her, and we'd be downstairs in Family Court again, but this time I took a deep, deep breath and forced myself to overlook it.

"OK, Mavis," I said as calmly as I could. "I think I get why you want to protest Herbal Excellence, but can't you just write them a letter or something? Or you could just not buy their shampoo and stuff. That would show you aren't supporting them."

Mavis put the book down and dropped her face in her hands. I thought she was going to cry, but when she lifted it again, she said,

"I know you don't get it, Camille, and I'm tired of trying to explain it. So when WPPT mentions it on the radio, I won't have to anymore, because everyone in the whole entire state will be boycotting them."

I was hotter than James Brown's Hot Pants. Here I was trying to understand my sister. My twin. Trying to get her point of view. Well, she didn't deserve my understanding if she could go behind my back and broadcast our business to the world.

"You called the radio station and told them about this? Where is that masking tape?" I asked her, searching under her bed and in our closet. "You want to drive a wedge between us? Well, congratulations 'cause you just did."

CHAPTER 16

For the next few days, our house was pretty quiet. I wasn't speaking to Mavis, and she wasn't speaking to me. I told Mama and Daddy what happened so they wouldn't think it was my fault. They put Mavis on punishment, and she had to give up her internship. I hated that for her, but it was her own fault for disobeying her sentence. She was supposed to cease and desist, but instead she persisted, and now she's paying the price.

Daddy made her call WPPT and recant, but they refused, saying they'd done their own research and would see us in New Castle.

"And as far as the internship is concerned," Mavis said with her head held high, "I learned all I could from them, and I was ready to quit."

I knew that was a lie, but that was Mavis, as stubborn as a mule in a mud bath. So I didn't bother to tell her Mama and Daddy's story or show her the letter from Dear Addy. But I had changed my views on the contest. Yes, I still wanted to win, since I'd never won anything, but not if it meant being labeled an airhead, and not if it meant embarrassing my family, like WPPT was about to do. So I decided to find a way to kill two birds with

one stone: get the fat cats at Herbal Excellence to do the right
thing and stay in the competition. Besides, Julius wouldn't want
his future wife to get mixed up in any racial unrest, so I had a
duty to him and to our future. Yep. I also decided that him being
a nerd wasn't all bad—especially since he was a *cute* nerd.
Besides, Mama and Daddy always said smart people got good
jobs, and I wanted my husband to be on it, doggone it.

Armed with a new outlook, I bided my time, knowing
that any day now, the whole town would hear the *real* story
about me, my sister, and Herbal Excellence.

Despite my new plan, I'd have to work with her somehow,
scary as that sounded. And just when I thought things were
going to be alright, we got a rude awakening just one week
before the big announcement:

We were lying on our twin beds, as usual, listening to the
crackly reception of the radio station—WPPT-AM—
broadcasting from somewhere south of Aliquippa, when the
DJ stopped the music and said to his listeners, 'I just heard
something I got to lay on you.'

I rolled onto my elbows, and Mavis reached for the knob
to turn it up.

*"Hey all you guys and gals out there in radio land, there's a
funky situation brewing up the street, in the little town of New
Castle, PA—"*

"Little town?" I complained. "What does he think
Aliquippa is?"

"S-h-h-h, Camille. I want to hear this."

I wrinkled my nose at her. "Why? You already know what
he's gonna say."

*"…from what my sources tell me, the big shots that make
Herbal Excellence shampoo don't use black people in their
advertisements—"*

"See? He's got it all wrong. *I'm* black—" I protested.

"Will you stop talking?"

"*...and to make up for it, they've gone and chosen a redbone with long straight hair to represent them...*"

I smacked Mavis on the behind. "Did you say that about me? He called me a *redbone*."

"No, I just said you were light-skinned, that's all—"

"Oh, and did you bother to tell him we look EXACTLY ALIKE?"

She put her finger to her lips and basically ignored me.

"*...so WPPT has decided to take our show on the road for the big reveal. That's right. We'll be broadcasting live from New Castle on May 10 so you don't miss a single bit of what's about to go down up there...*"

I jumped up and switched the radio off.

"What'd you do that for?" Mavis complained. "He was about to get back to the jams."

"And I'm about five minutes off from jamming you up. Do you know what this means? Mama and Daddy are gonna be there, and probably the whole school. You're gonna make us the laughingstock of the Keystone State."

A frown crossed Mavis' face, and for a split second I thought she might be repentant after all she'd done.

Not on your life.

"We won't be anybody's laughingstock," she said with evil in her eyes. "Not if you agree to my *next* plan..."

And that's when things got *real* crazy.

———

As soon as Mavis laid out her vision for what she called The Hair Dare, a boulder sank in my gut. Her plan: for us to switch hairstyles on contest day so that she could trick Herbal Excellence into changing their policy. She assured me that our parents didn't have to know AND that when they *did* find out, they'd be proud of her.

I didn't buy it, but I took solace in the fact that her punishment for this latest crime would be a popcorn and Pepsi moment I didn't want to miss. So I kept my trap shut and my mind open.

Mavis insisted we test the switch on family and friends first in order to be ready for the big day. How would we ever pull it off? Trading places in school was bad enough, but at home, too? Mama wouldn't permit it, and on top of that, Daddy could always tell us apart—no matter how our hair looked. There was no way we could fool him.

"This is the best, most genius idea I've ever come up with, isn't it?"

Mavis was about as excited as an army of ants on a rotten apple. You should have seen her running between the bedroom and bathroom, pulling out clothes and hair products. She was really serious. I was really scared.

"All we have to do is be each other for a few days and see if anyone can tell," she said, counting the number of curlers in my vanity drawer. "The only problem I see is getting your hair into an Afro, but I think I can do it."

"You're forgetting we tried that once before. My head looked like a teased-up mess, and getting those knots out wasn't exactly a picnic."

Mavis searched through the box of combs and picks in her nightstand. They were all shapes and sizes. I hadn't realized she needed that many combs to maintain an Afro, but then Mavis was always a sucker for a sale. Like the time she came home with fourteen mirrors from her ex-employer, World of Crafts.

"We can create a psychedelic vibe in here," she'd said, pointing to our perfectly pink bedroom wall.

Those mirrors—which took every bit of her allowance and

some of mine—came in all shapes and sizes. But her silly idea to turn our room into a 60s love-in didn't last. That was because after Mama got one look at it, she laid down the law.

"Get those hippie-dippy things off my wall," she told Mavis.

So, of course, they went. Good thing she didn't see the lava lamp.

Mama didn't seem to have a problem with peace signs, though. Guess they made her hopeful about Daddy and the end of the war. So Mavis found a bunch of little stick-on peace signs and formed them into one giant peace sign for our perfectly pink bedroom wall. They're still sticking perfectly well.

"Okay, are you ready to go to the Motherland?" Mavis asked, walking me into the bathroom. She was holding an extra-wide, extra-large comb in one hand and a bottle of hairspray in the other. And that wasn't the worst part. It was her eyes. They had that wild, mad scientist, Dr. Jekyll thing going on (or was it Mr. Hyde?) Whichever it was, she looked more like a scaredresser than a hairdresser.

"I'm not so sure about this, Mavis," I said, sinking into the chair she'd pulled out of Mama's bedroom. "What if it turns out like the last time? Nobody will believe I'm you if that happens."

"Stop worrying. I didn't really know what I was doing back then," she said, referring to the incident that took place just a year ago. "This time I have better equipment. I'll tease it up real good and then spray it as I go. Last time I didn't pack it with water. Water will make it thicker, like mine."

Mavis didn't even finish reassuring me before her grubby little hands were all over my head. It wouldn't have worked anyway. The reassurance, I mean. No matter what she said, I knew this was a very, very bad idea.

Picture me sitting in literal fear as my long, silky mane

was transformed into a thick, knotted, Dippity-Do mess. I looked like the Wicked Witch of Wild Kingdom.

"It's almost there," Mavis said with a nervousness that made me even more afraid.

How did I let her talk me into this?

No twins I knew ever tried to pull a stunt like this. Then again, no twins I knew had un-identical hair. My fate was sealed.

Since things hadn't gone quite as well as she'd planned, Mavis suggested I better not watch the rest of the Makeover from Muppet Land. You think Oscar the Grouch had bad hair days? He was a beauty queen compared to me.

"Can I open my eyes now, and when I do, am I going to vomit?" I kept my hands over my mouth as I asked this question, just in case I did vomit.

But when I opened my eyes to see the finished product, I had to admit, Mavis had worked a real miracle.

"How'd you do it? I look like Pam Grier."

"More like Vonetta McGee. Her skin color is a closer match."

"Vonetta works," I said about the star of the new movie, *Shaft in Africa*. She was very pretty no matter how she wore her hair.

For the first time in our lives, Mavis and I actually looked like real twins—hair and all. I could feel a huge lump in my throat as my sister hugged me, and I knew she was crying because I felt drops on my shoulders and heard a few sniffs.

Then we pulled apart, laughed together, and bounced on our twin beds to figure out the rest of the plan.

"Now, it's your turn," I said, knowing that our *identical* identical twinness wouldn't last very long. "We've got to straighten your hair next."

"That, my sister, will be the easy part. The hard part will be to get you to act like me."

"What do you mean?" I said, feeling my eyebrows stiffen.
"I have enough toughness in my personality to stand up to
the downest militant teenager." Though I was sure "downest"
was not a word. Come to think of it, I was sure "down"
wasn't either, at least not the way we used it.

"No, no. You don't get it," Mavis said. "You can't just look
like me to be down; you have to sound like me and do the
things I do. That's what's going to fool everyone. You have to
be me in every way."

She sat me in front of the vanity mirror.

"First you have to practice fluffing your Afro."

"Fluffing my Afro? I'm not going to spend hours sticking
this pitchfork in my head like you do—"

"Just think," Mavis interrupted, dancing around the room
in a daydreamy kind of way.

"As me, you'll be able to find out all kinds of things about
yourself without anyone even knowing it." She floated
around some more and then stood behind me in the mirror.
"You could even get the lowdown on some boy you might be
liking," she said, winking at me in the mirror, "because he
will think you are me." She smiled wide at my reflection.

I tried to look uninterested so that Mavis wouldn't think I
was cornered.

After all, we were twins. And come to think of it, if I did
approach Julius as Mavis, I could pump him for information
on how he really felt about *me*.

One thing I loved about Mavis, besides her being my twin,
was her sinister, sneaky, unscrupulous mind.

I picked up her box of combs.

"When I fluff, should I use the metal pick or the plastic
one?"

CHAPTER 17

We decided that right after the contest, we'd go back to being our old selves. I missed myself already, wondering how I was going to live under this beehive for the next few days. But if it helped us teach Herbal Excellence a lesson, it was worth every knot, snarl, and snag I'd have to comb out.

I spent what was left of the night taking a hot comb to my sister's hair. I closed my parents' bedroom door on the way down to the kitchen so they wouldn't smell the smoke. Pressed hair has a very distinctive smell that every Black woman knows.

"Ouch," Mavis winced. "Watch it."

I wasn't very good at pressing, so I tried to be careful.

Pressing is an art. You need a steady hand, or else you can burn someone, like I did.

Having naturally straight hair, I never had to use the hot comb, which got me to thinking about genes. I'd never understood how genes worked. I mean, how could Mavis and I look identical but have such different hair? My biology teacher had us do an exercise once where we figured out why more people had brown eyes than blue eyes, but he never explained genes. Most twins were born with everything the same, so we must have gotten some freaky gene that made our hair different. In fact, I didn't know any other kids like us. We might have been the only ones in the entire universe.

But whatever the gene had done to us, it only took a little heat to whip Mavis' 'fro into submission. When I finished, she looked like me. The old me, that is—silky and straight.

It was showtime.

"Look," Mavis marveled. "Now I am you and you are me." Mavis flounced around the room swinging her new hair. She couldn't seem to keep her hands off it. Until now, she'd kept her 'fro because it was the style and because she didn't want to make the hot comb a habit. The hairdresser said it would break her ends.

Then I got to thinking, "Instead of the hair dare, we should call it Hairism. You know, like racism only—"

"I get it." Mavis put her finger to her chin. "I like it. Hairism. That's what we are trying to defeat."

Mavis plopped in front of the mirror again, still admiring her new do.

We decided to test Mama and Daddy with our plan to fool Herbal Excellence. When Mavis and I sat down to breakfast before catching the bus, Mama was waiting in the kitchen with a full spread. Like I said before, things changed after Daddy came home.

Most days Mavis and I just ate cereal or some toast or something. But that morning we had a choice of all our favorites. There were blueberry muffins and fruit, which to me was not a real breakfast, but Mavis loved blueberries. Eggs scrambled with American cheese and thick-sliced country bacon cooked to a crisp—my absolute favorite.

Mama was fluttering all through the kitchen, putting down muffins, meat, and margarine. Then she started dishing it up: eggs and bacon for me, muffins and fruit for Mavis.

"I've got to take your father to the VA at eight o'clock sharp, so eat up."

Two plates, two forks, and two napkins appeared before us.

"There you are," Mama said, after she served us both.

Mavis and I looked at each other at the exact same time.

"What is it?" She asked us, pulling on her trench coat. "Did I forget something?"

"No," we said in unison.

"Hello, my little angels," Daddy said as he walked through the kitchen, snapped up a slice of bacon, and headed for the garage door. "Don't dilly-dally, or you'll miss your bus."

Mama ran out the door, and we sat at the kitchen table staring at our mixed-up plates.

"You see," Mavis said. "She gave you muffins, and she gave me your eggs. That proves she didn't know us."

I slid my eggs from under my sister's nose and started eating.

"Mama knows I hate eggs with cheese," Mavis said, "so why else would she give them to me?"

I shrugged and pushed in a few more spoonfuls.

"I'm telling you, Camille. She was fooled. I can't wait to get to school and see everyone else's reaction."

If I hadn't had a mouthful of food, I would have told Mavis that she was overreacting about Mama. It was an honest mistake. But this was important to Mavis, and since I was on her team this time around, I kept quiet. Of course, the food helped.

We got our books and paper-sack lunches, then ran out to wait for the bus. Mavis pulled her hair behind her ears, trying to get it out of the way so she could get that hideous green backpack over her shoulder.

"Mavis, what are you doing?" I asked, noticing she was

not acting like me at all. "Give me that backpack." I handed her my suede shoulder bag.

"Oh." Mavis quickly traded bags with me. She even took off the headband she was wearing, which was so not my style.

"And you thought *I* was going to mess this up?" I said.

"I goofed. I'll get it right tomorrow," she said.

"If this goes on until tomorrow," I said.

She'd also forgotten to switch perfume with me until she smelled herself on the way out the door.

"Go wash your wrists before the bus comes," I scolded, wishing I didn't have to smell like a lemon. That was her favorite perfume, Love's Lemon Scent. I always wore Jovan Musk Oil because it had a deep woodsy smell that didn't arrive ten minutes before I did.

By the time we reached the bus stop, we had successfully become each other. Or so I'd hoped.

"Hi, Mavis, Hi, Camille," said every kid who usually spoke to us on the bus. Even the ones who ignored us didn't seem to notice our charade. Test number one: passed. But I was sure we'd get busted once we got to our first class.

Mavis and I didn't have all our subjects together, so I was getting nervous about how to respond to her teachers and classmates.

"Just focus on the board and your book or paper or whatever they have you doing," Mavis said. "Don't say anything you normally say, and don't do anything you normally do."

I let out a breathy sigh, which, when translated, means you're full of hot air.

"You know what I mean. Just act like me."

"Mavis, I don't know how you act when I'm not around you. This is dumb, and I'm probably going to end up looking that way, too."

"Okay then, be yourself. Just don't act like yourself and you'll be fine."

"Bye, Mavis. See you at lunch."

As I walked through the halls, I could swear kids were staring at my hair. This Afro looked decent, but it didn't look like my sister's. That worried me, especially when I saw Gerald coming down the hall. Immediately, I went the other way.

"Mavis," I heard him say.

Shoot.

I made like I was going to the girl's bathroom, but he caught me before I could get in.

"Hey, my African queen, what's your hurry?"

"I gotta go to the bathroom," I said, keeping my head down so all he could see was hair. If he'd seen my face, I would've given myself away.

"Well, uh, why don't I wait for you, and we can walk to Miss Greer's together?"

I could feel the sweat dampening my scalp. It was making me itch, and I wanted to scratch.

Why didn't he just get lost?

I tried to inch my way into the bathroom. My neck was hurting from holding my head down. On top of that, my scalp still itched, and I was dying to scratch it.

Luckily, the bell rang, and Gerald sped off, but not before promising to see me at lunch.

"Great," I said to only me.

In the bathroom, I ran into the first available stall and let my fingers do the walking, but they were getting lost trying to maneuver through all the hair protruding from my head.

It was then that I understood why those with Afros always carried long-toothed combs. I mean picks.

I have to remember that. They call them picks, not combs.

The term 'pick' made sense to me now because I sure was picking through my head trying to soothe the sensation.

By the time my crisis ended, I was late for class.

Darn it.

Now I was sure to stand out. I got there in time for some kind of writing assignment, so I slid to the back of the room and took a seat. Mavis had given me notes the night before for all her subjects. In Miss Greer's class they were finishing up an essay on Alexander Hamilton.

Lucky for Mavis, history was one of my better subjects. My teacher was Mr. Henderson, and we'd done this exercise last week.

After class, I filed out behind the other kids, but Miss Greer called me aside.

"Mavis, you were late. What was the problem *this* time, and where is your hall pass?"

"I—I was sick in the bathroom when the bell rang. It won't happen again."

"You were sick last week too when you were late. Does your mother know about these sudden bouts of sickness?"

"No, ma'am. Maybe I had the stomach flu? It's going around, you know."

Miss Greer seemed puzzled.

"You told me last week it was food poisoning."

I gulped.

"Get to class before you're late for that one, too. We'll discuss this tomorrow."

"Yes, ma'am."

It figures. My very first class, and things were already going wrong. Mavis and food poisoning? That girl has never had food poisoning in her life. I should know. Our stomachs are ironclad. Of course, I've never had the stomach flu either, but I had to say something. Mavis never mentioned being tardy—regularly tardy at that. Now I had something on her I could use when I needed a favor. I could tell Mama—and Daddy—all about it, and I got it straight from the teacher's mouth.

Second period was gym. Mavis was in that class with me.

"Look at your hair," she said, fluffing it out with the comb (I mean pick) she'd left in her locker. "How many times have I told you to keep it shaped up?"

"Shaped up? I'm about ready to ship out. Do you know I almost got sent to the principal's office over your class-skipping shenanigans?"

"Stop talking like Daddy. I bet even he doesn't know what that word means."

"Mavis, I'm serious. This is not working. We should've waited to do this on contest day—"

"It *is* working. We need to know that it's going to work in front of the whole town, and this is the only way. And wait until I tell you what happened last period in *your* class."

———

IN GYM, we were finishing the modern dance routines where everyone was paired up. Mavis and I were assigned with two other girls, and today it was our turn. That's when the reality hit me.

"Oh, no," I said out loud, not meaning to, but it flew out of my mouth.

"What?" Mavis gave me that worried look she always gets when she thinks I'm getting sick or something. "Are you all right?"

"Mavis," I whispered, "we are in T-R-O-U-B-L-E." I spelled it because I didn't want to say it. "We forgot that you are dancing with Janice, and I am dancing with Francine. Do you know what that means?"

Mavis's face suddenly turned whiter than a ghost. Then

she smacked her head with the palm of her hand. We were sunk, but as always, Mavis had a plan.

"Well, uh, you saw me practice with Janice, so do whatever it is you remember seeing us do."

Wrong answer.

"Are you nuts? I didn't see all of your routine, and you didn't see *any* of ours." She crossed her arms and let her lip poke out. "So much for the Hair Dare," I said.

I could already visualize the disaster that was about to take place—in front of 20 girls who would end up blabbing about it all over the school: how Mavis and Camille tried to change places and got caught when their dance routines flopped.

The first two girls got up and danced to Elton John, which surprised me because we were told not to use songs with words in them. They wore yellow ribbons in their hair to match the song title.

I looked over at Mavis because she was up next with Francine.

"Don't be all uptight," I told her. "Just do whatever Francine does."

Mavis' eyes bugged at me as she got up to take her place on the gym floor.

Francine stood on the mat in her blue tights and bodysuit. We had agreed to wear a pink belt to match. But when Mavis got up, she was dressed in purple, like Janice, my new partner.

How did we forget to switch outfits?

"This is terrible," I said to myself. I wanted to die right then and there.

"Miss Marconi," the gym teacher said to Mavis. "I believe you and your sister have on the wrong outfits." All the girls laughed. "Why don't you go back to the locker room and change into the right ones? I'll let the others go ahead of you until you get back."

Immediately we ran out of the gym, and the laughter, of course, ran after us.

"I cannot believe you let this happen," Mavis said. "You know I can't remember everything."

I stood there with my hands on my hips and attitude on my lips. "Are you for real? This is *my* fault? If it wasn't for your little experiment, we'd be in there right now getting this stupid modern dance jive over with."

So Mavis and I quickly switched outfits. But on our way back I worried about how Mavis was going to do with Francine. Unlike me, she'd never seen our routine because Francine and I practiced at her house. It was going to be the longest gym class in history.

Mavis rejoined Francine on the mat. She watched her strike a pose, so she did the same. Then the music started, and my heart stopped.

They danced to an instrumental called "Love's Theme" by Barry White, 'the Maestro,' as the kids called him. It was a pretty song, and so I decided to close my eyes and listen so I wouldn't have to see my sister failing miserably at the dance. Every now and then I'd hear yelps and giggles, and I knew Mavis was not keeping up very well. But it served her right for coming up with this stupendously stupid swap.

"Thank you, ladies," the gym teacher said with a lot less enthusiasm than she'd had for the earlier dancers. "You all had weeks to prepare for this; unfortunately, it didn't show."

All the girls burst out laughing, and I could tell Francine was not pleased.

"Thanks for nothing, Camille," she said to Mavis. I knew then that when this little charade was over, I'd have to play the Clean Up Woman to get a lot of things back to normal.

"Mavis and Janice, you're next," the teacher said.

I followed Janice to the mat, and like Mavis, I did whatever my partner did. Lucky for me I'd remembered a little bit of their routine since Janice had come to the house to go over it once with Mavis. I wasn't the greatest, but I got by. Her arm went left. Mine went left. Her leg went right. Mine went right. She twirled. I twirled. Honestly, it was a lot more like follow-the-leader and a lot less like synchronized swimming, but when we were done, at least we didn't get cracked on. That was all I could hope for, so I was satisfied to have dodged that bullet.

Of course, the next day would be worse.

CHAPTER 18

At school, I spent some of my free time with Mavis, but under normal circumstances I hung with the Jewels. I felt a sinking in my chest thinking about all the fun I was going to miss with them while pretending to be Mavis—swapping cute ideas, discussing our unique hair issues, and sharing the latest styles we'd read in the glamour magazines. Shallow or not, I still liked the Jewels, so this switch wasn't going to earn me any brownie points. For instance, while I was sitting in the lunchroom waiting for Mavis, I watched Stephanie and Cynthia take seats a few tables away. So, I smiled in their direction, and you won't believe what they did. Gave me the cold shoulder. Me. Camille Marconi—the queen of the Cool Jewels. Did they think they were all that? Puh-leez. It had only been a week since we were sitting together, talking about the new jumbo hair rollers at the five and dime store, and we all agreed to get some as soon as we could save up enough of our allowances. Now they were acting like I didn't even exist. I mean, I get it. I am wearing an Afro. That's when I started wondering how they treated Mavis when I wasn't around. All of a sudden, I felt kind of sad.

I must have looked pretty torn up when Mavis came to sit down. But instead of sitting, she stood there holding up a carton of milk she'd gotten to go with her sandwich, like she was about to endorse the benefits of Vitamin D.

"What's your problem?" she asked, still holding up the milk carton.

"Oh, nothing," I said.

Then her eyes followed mine to the girls a few tables away.

"Oh-h-h-h, OK. So, they aren't speaking to you, are they?" She finally said, and then she turned around and waved to them.

"What are you doing?" I practically yelled. "I don't want them coming over here and—"

But it was too late. Cynthia was already headed our way.

I thought I was going to die when Mavis flung her hair behind her with the hand that was not holding the milk carton.

"Hey girl," Mavis said with a familiarity reserved for truly close friends, which they definitely were not. "Love those Shirley Temple curls on you."

"My mom had it done," Cynthia said, oozing with sickening self-conceit. I thought I was going to throw up. Until that very moment, I never realized how dumb we must've sounded to other kids. Being Mavis was opening up a whole new side of things for me.

"Aren't you going to speak to Mavis?" Mavis asked Cynthia.

"Oh, sure, hi there. I mean, right on." Then she laughed out loud. "Camille, I'll talk to you later, girl."

Cynthia walked back to her table. I sat there and said nothing. That's right. I, Camille Marconi—the one with the curls that shamed all the girls—had lost my courage to be cocky.

"Did you see how she acted?" Mavis said after she sat down. "That is exactly what I'm talking about."

"Even though she dissed me—pretending to be you—doesn't mean she has hairism."

I knew I was trying to justify the whole incident, and I was mad that they ignored me, but I refused to believe it was completely over the hair. Stephanie and Cynthia weren't into activism. But as I watched them, I finally realized that what the Jewels *were* into was pretty phony.

"I'm telling you," Mavis said proudly, "this is one of my best, most genius ideas."

———

In Mavis' next class, everybody in the room looked scared. It seems most of them weren't ready for the math test, and the way they were talking to me, they didn't expect Mavis to be ready either.

"Oh, I got this," I said. "My super-smart sister Camille taught me everything I need to know. I won't be scratching anything out. In fact, my paper's going to be so clean you'll think I washed it in Tide."

Yep, I said it, and I didn't care that they all gasped. Mavis may not talk like that, but I couldn't let that moment get away. Finally, something I could enjoy about this bait and switch. Being able to boost my rep in front of the other kids might actually make this trip worthwhile.

I was all fired up to brag to Mavis about it in study hall, but before I could, we had a visitor. Gerald eased up on us and plopped himself down next to me—the fake Mavis.

"Peace, my Nubian princess."

The *real* Mavis smirked but tried to hide it behind her history book. Yes, I had to admit it; this was my sister's best, most genius idea, and that's when it hit me. I could use this situation to carry out my own plan. Yes. My *own* plan to stick it to the man!

CHAPTER 19

The morning of the contest program, I got the jitters. Not only because I felt like an imposter in that hair, but I also felt like an imposter in my own skin. But I knew what I had to do, and I intended to do it.

"It's going to be fine," she said, fluffing my hair out with her fisted Afro pick. "All you have to do is watch."

Since she wouldn't tell me what she had in mind, I decided to test her out with this line:

"I think we should both go up there with straight hair; then they will *really* be fooled."

But Mavis didn't bite.

"I have my speech all ready for those fat cats," she announced with glee. "After I'm done, they won't have a choice. They'll have to change their ways."

Once everyone was ready, we all got into Daddy's deuce and a quarter and drove to the event site: Cascade Park.

Cascade was the only park in New Castle, and people came from miles around to ride the giant roller coaster and the other rides featured at the park. There was a big area with picnic tables and a few covered sections with concrete floors.

One of those is where Herbal Excellence planned to make their announcement.

When we drove under the arched entrance and onto the graveled driveway, we saw all kinds of wires running from a truck. It had WPPT plastered across the side in giant letters. Mavis had sent the DJ my picture, so when he spotted us, he came right over—him and his microphone.

"Ladies and gentlemen, the twins have arrived, along with their mother and father. Hey, Mr. Marconi, can we ask you a few questions?"

Daddy waved him away with a sheepish grin. "You can talk to my daughters instead." Then he and Mama strolled to the covered area to find a seat.

But when the DJ stepped to us to get an interview, Mavis put up her hand. "We can't talk to you until after the event. Contest rules." Then she took my hand and dragged me to the covered area.

As she pulled me along, I stared at her in amazement. Was that my sister—the pigheaded publicity hound—turning down a live interview with our favorite radio station? Something was definitely amiss, which got me a little worried.

"Hey, wait a minute," the DJ said, trailing us like we were a big scoop. "I've got tons of listeners waiting to boycott Herbal Excellence; they're waiting for a word from you."

Mavis turned to him and said, "Patience, my brother, patience. You won't be disappointed."

Then she turned on her heel, with me in tow, and made a beeline for the stage.

Did I say how totally confused my sister had me? I emphasize 'totally.' So I decided to do what she told that DJ: to be patient. After all, with our parents in the audience, Mavis wouldn't dare try something stupid. But I hated being on pins and needles. I had to put *my* plan into action...and soon.

As we approached the stage, a woman spotted us and motioned for us to join her behind the curtain they'd erected.

"Camille," she said to Mavis, not knowing we'd switched identities. "Come with me."

"Wait," Mavis said, taking my hand. "What about my sister? I want her to stay."

The woman frowned, then nodded, and led us both to a makeup person to give Mavis a touching up.

"Just follow my lead," Mavis whispered to me from the wooden director's chair where she sat. "Everything is going to be fine."

While they put the finishing touches on my sisterly sidekick, I peeked from behind the curtain, and what did I see? It was just like the DJ described: tons of people were out there—on benches and folding chairs or just standing around waiting. Waiting for us. It was amazing, and my heart thumped at the thought of being the center of all that attention.

"It's time." The woman said to Mavis, and I followed them to the curtain, but instead of going out front, I stayed behind.

When Mavis appeared, people jeered. Some made catcalls and threw fists into the air. It was that straight hair. I felt for her, especially when they began to chant:

The woman ran to the microphone to quiet the spectators. "Please allow us to announce our winner. If you want to protest, please do it quietly."

Some continued to chant even louder, and others joined in until the DJ from WPPT came to the stage. He raised his hands to the crowd. "My people, let the lady do her thing; afterward we can do ours." His words caused cheers and Black Power fists. He bowed to the woman as he left the stage, which incited a few fits of laughter. The woman's face said she was not impressed, but she got it together and continued with the program.

"Thank you," she said. "And now, after a long and careful search for the right girl to represent Herbal Excellence in our next TV commercial, allow me to present to you Miss Camille Marconi."

Most of the audience clapped, and Mama and Daddy stood, but some were still unhappy, and you could hear it in the various grunts and groans way in the back.

The mayor of New Castle showed up, too. He came onto the stage and congratulated my sister.

"As mayor of the great city of New Castle, let me be the first to publicly say that we are so proud of you, Camille. And I also want to tell all the other young girls who took part in this contest that we are proud of you, too. And to those of you who were less pleased about this choice, let me just say that we respect your views. Please respect theirs." Then he shook my sister's hand while cameras flashed.

Now it was time for my twin to speak and for me to put *my* plan into action. The woman smiled at Mavis and waved her to the microphone. I tried to keep my composure, hoping I could hold out long enough to let Mavis at least get to the mic. I stood behind the curtain, watching and waiting. I peeked out to see Mama and Daddy, then crossed my fingers and toes that all went well.

Mavis got to the middle of the stage and adjusted the microphone.

Where she learned that, I'll never know

Then she said:

"First of all, I want to say thank you for giving me this platform to say how I *really* feel about Herbal Excellence and this contest…"

My hand flew to my mouth, and I went into a cold sweat.

I couldn't let Mavis do this, so I dashed onto the stage and took the mic.

"...Hi...uh...that was my sister," I said, clutching the mic, which created loud squeaks of feedback. My eyes darted from the confused crowd to Mavis, but I continued. "My twin sister, Mavis—"

"What are you doing?" The woman from Herbal Excellence rushed to my side.

"*I* am Camille Marconi," I announced.

The crowd went wild, and a chant began, "Afros Forever, Afros Forever."

Mavis stood there, her mouth open, like she could not believe what she saw.

"My sister was just trying to help me, but," I said, my eyes still on her. "But I have to do this myself." I took in a deep breath and let it all out. "This contest has taught me a lot of things: about myself, about my family, and about my duty as a young black woman..."

More cheers. I could see Daddy and Mama trying to shush the people seated around them and, at the same time, trying to figure out the hair switcheroo.

"...at first, I wanted to be in this contest because I had never won anything. Ever. And this seemed like a great opportunity for me. But then, my sister helped me to appreciate that some things are just not worth it, so we switched hairstyles to prove a point. *Our* point..."

I grabbed Mavis' hand. Not to keep her from doing anything crazy, but to keep her near me.

"...she wanted to protest Herbal Excellence because they do not feature Afros in their ads. And, at first, I didn't think that was such a big deal." I lowered my lids. "But now I have to admit that this is unfair to girls everywhere who do not have straight hair—"

The crowd went wild, and the DJ from WPPT tried to get

them settled down. That's when the woman from Herbal Excellence started to approach again. "Please let me finish," I said to her, and the crowd agreed, booing her away from the microphone.

"...I know now that what my sister was fighting for was bigger than just a contest, and with the help of my parents, my conscience, and a very special person, I was able to do something about it—"

Now Mama had her hand over her mouth. Daddy put his arm around her. And, of course, the woman from Herbal Excellence tried again to reach the microphone, but I held tight because the best part was yet to come.

"Now," I said. "I have to introduce that very special person. Someone who has promised to change the policy at Herbal Excellence so that we can all truly say, 'Afro or straight, Herbal Excellence is great.' Mr. Jacob Ayers."

Silence fell on the crowd as a tall, older man came from out of the audience and took center stage. He came and stood by me.

"Who is that?" Mavis whispered.

"He owns Herbal Excellence," I said. "I'll tell you about it later."

"Thank you, Camille," Mr. Ayers said. "You *are* Camille, right?" Everyone laughed, and I nodded. "Hello everyone, and thank you all for coming. As she said, my name is Jacob Ayers, and I am the president of the Curall company, makers of Herbal Excellence and many other hair products for women and girls. I got a phone call from this little lady telling me how upset she and her sister were that we did not feature Afros in our ads. Well, I investigated that and discovered that my marketing team was in fact discriminating against Afro-wearing girls in their model search. So I put a stop to it, and I am happy to announce that both Camille *and* Mavis will star in our upcoming commercial with the new slogan that Mavis herself created."

Mavis' mouth fell open again, and I hugged her so hard I nearly smothered her with my big hair.

We waved at Mama and Daddy. She was crying, and Daddy was trying to calm her down.

"And one more thing," Mr. Ayers continued. "Many of you may be wondering why we chose New Castle for our model search out of all the other cities in America. Well, I'll tell you. For those who do not know, I grew up in this area—Mahoningtown, to be exact—and I would not have chosen any other place to find the perfect girl for this company."

I scanned the audience for the DJ from WPPT, because no one was protesting now. Instead, cheers and claps were all I heard. When I spotted him, he was standing by his truck talking into his microphone, no doubt broadcasting the entire thing to everyone between here and the east side of Aliquippa. It was truly a far-out day, and all Mavis kept saying was, "Right on, my sister, right on."

CHAPTER 20

At the end of the show, Mavis and I rejoined Mama and Daddy in the audience, and after we gave hugs all around, I peeled my eyes to find Julius. I thought I'd seen him while I was backstage, but it wasn't easy seeing that far away. I still needed to get those glasses because we never made it to the eye doctor.

My family headed to the car, and I kept searching. The DJ from WPPT was still by his truck, this time interviewing Mr. Ayers. Most of the crowd had left or gone off to other parts of the park. Mama and Daddy wanted to get corn dogs before we left, but Mavis and I hated corn dogs, so we waited by the car.

"Let's get on the Comet," Mavis suggested. "We haven't been on that roller coaster since we were little."

Mavis knew how scared I was of roller coasters, and the Comet went up 65 terrifying feet.

"It's a special occasion, and I've got so much energy I need to release it," Mavis urged, "so let's go."

The line to get on the Comet was not as long as I'd hoped, so I couldn't use that as an excuse to not take the 65-foot plunge. The closer we got to the ticket booth, the more jittery I became. Then a voice came up behind me.

"You guys were great today." It was Julius, and Gerald was with him.

"Hey Mavis, my African Queen." Gerald said, moving in front of me to get to Mavis. "Interesting hair," he said in a joking manner. "Miss your natural, though."

She tapped him and laughed. "Variety is the spice of life, my brother. My twin taught me that."

"I can dig it," he said.

My skin was still crawling when we got our tickets and headed to the boxcars that would take my breath and my heart to another level.

"I got an idea," Gerald said. "I can ride with Mavis, and Julius, you can ride with Camille."

"Thanks for giving me permission," he said. "But I already planned to do that."

My eyes grew three sizes. Julius, my dream date, was going to take this ride with me. You know I had to be cool now, even though I was scared to death.

We all climbed in, buckled up, and as soon as the seats began to move, I felt the tension in my legs, like when you're a passenger in a car but you smash an imaginary brake.

"Don't be scared," Julius said, "I won't let you fall." He scooted closer to me, and as soon as we hit the first dip, I screamed so loud I nearly burst an eardrum.

Julius wrapped his arms around me, and I pushed my face into his chest. Eyes closed tight. My heart raced. I could hear Mavis and Gerald in front of us laughing and screaming with delight. When the coaster slowed down, I panted.

"It's almost over," Julius said, trying to comfort me. He was being so sweet, and I was being such a baby.

As the coaster reached the top of the next dip, I felt faint.

Good thing I hadn't eaten, or else it would be all over Julius' lap.

OOOOOOHHHHHHHH

I squeezed his waist so hard I could hear him gasping for air. But in an instant, it was all over, and the cars rolled slowly back to the starting point.

"Wow, that was fun," Mavis said, standing outside my car. I couldn't move for a few minutes, and she laughed. "Come on, Camille, it wasn't that bad."

Julius helped me out and stayed close by until my legs stopped wobbling.

The guys walked with us to the car, where Mama and Daddy stood finishing off their dogs.

"See you at school Monday?" Julius asked.

"Sure," I said.

Then he and Gerald went their own way.

———

"WHAT A DAY THIS HAS BEEN," Mavis said, up in our bedroom. I sat at the vanity with a pick and a comb, trying to carefully part my hair so I could smooth it out and get back to normal.

"Let me help," Mavis said, taking over. "I promise I won't hurt."

She took her time getting out all the tangles while I winced to prepare for any oncoming pain. "So how did you find the number for Mr. Ayers?"

"It was on the back of the shampoo bottle at Hite's," I said. "They didn't let me speak to him right off; I guess my crying helped." I lowered my eyes, and Mavis squeezed me from behind.

"I'm glad you came around to my way of thinking," she said, her face glowing. "Now we're going to be in a brand spanking new commercial, and on TV, too." Then Mavis turned her attention to our clock radio. "I wonder if they're talking about it on WPPT?"

When Mavis finished getting all the knots out of my hair, we sat on my bed, where I let my body fall backward onto the pillow. I was beat. But in a good way. I'd just had my first date with Julius; *plus*, both Mavis and I were going to be famous. I leaned over to switch on the radio, but she stopped me.

"Before we do that, can I say something?"

"If you're going to thank me, Mavis, please don't. I know I was being selfish about this whole protest thing, and it took me a while to realize what was right. I finally understand."

"I know you wanted to win, and it turns out we both won." We laughed. "Now, let's listen."

"…and that was the soulful sound of The Pointer Sisters with *Yes, We Can Can*, which seemed to be the theme at Cascade Park in New Castle earlier today, when identical twins, Camille and Mavis Marconi, convinced a shampoo company to feature Afros *and* straight hair in their ads. In fact, the twins will be featured in an upcoming commercial touting the new slogan, "Afro or straight, Herbal Excellence is great'."

Mavis and I gushed as the DJ broadcast about us to the world, or at least this half of the state of Pennsylvania.

"…but a new development could put the brakes on the two beauties. A lawsuit is expected to be filed in civil court next week that will ban the commercial from being aired, citing that the model search was rigged, and that Mavis Marconi was never a contestant…"

Mavis and I both jumped from the bed.

"What in the heck is he talking about?" Mavis complained. "Mr. Ayers has the right to use whomever he wants in his commercials." Mavis was getting hot under the collar, and me? I was speechless.

"...the parents of 14-year-old Lydia Hughes allege that Curall, the parent company of Herbal Excellence, misrepresented itself by going counter to the terms of its contest. They are suing for one million dollars—"

"Who is Lydia Hughes?" asked Mavis, and that's when it hit me.

"She was one of the girls at the second audition," I said, "but she didn't even want to be there—"

"Well, this is a bunch of mess," Mavis grumbled, the wheels turning in her eyes, "and if they think they can cheat Mavis Marconi out her one chance to walk through that tulip garden..."

I smack my palm to my forehead. *Here we go again.*

ABOUT THE AUTHOR

Faith Knight is a former TV news reporter who enjoys cooking, sewing and Bible education. She lives in North Carolina with her husband. You can follow her @therealknightauthor on TikTok and www. therealknightauthor.com.